...house.co.uk

D1136560

Corgi Yearling:

JOEY PIGZA SWALLOWED THE KEY
JOEY PIGZA LOSES CONTROL

What Would Joey Do?

Jack Gantos

Illustrated by Neal Layton

CORGI YEARLING BOOKS

For Anne and Mabel

WHAT WOULD JOEY DO?
A CORGI YEARLING BOOK 978 0 440 86521 6

Originally published in the USA by Farrar, Straus and Giroux
First published in Great Britain by Corgi Books,
an imprint of Random House Children's Books

This edition published 2003

3 5 7 9 10 8 6 4 2

Copyright © 2002 by Jack Gantos
Illustrations copyright © 2003 by Neal Layton

The right of Jack Gantos to be identified as the author of this
work has been asserted in accordance with the
Copyright, Designs and Patents Act 1988.

The Random House Group Limited supports The Forest Stewardship
Council (FSC), the leading international forest certification organisation
All our titles that are printed on Greenpeace approved FSC certified paper
carry the FSC logo. Our paper procurement policy can be found at:
www.rbooks.co.uk/environment

Set in 12.5/15.5 Century Schoolbook by
Falcon Oast Graphic Art Ltd.

Corgi Books are published by Random House Children's Books,
61–63 Uxbridge Road, London W5 5SA,
a division of The Random House Group Ltd.

Addresses for companies within The Random House Group Limited
can be found at:
www.randomhouse.co.uk/offices.htm

THE RANDOM HOUSE GROUP Limited Reg. No. 954009
www.**kids**at**randomhouse**.co.uk
A CIP catalogue record for this book is available from the
British Library.

Printed and bound in Great Britain by
CPI Cox & Wyman, Reading, Berkshire.

A Note from the Author

Joey Pigza is the hyperactive kid who in the first Joey Pigza book, *Joey Pigza Swallowed the Key*, is completely driven by his wild impulses, which lead him into trouble, both at school and at home. His family life is a mess, his teachers think he's a mess, and even Joey thinks he is a mess, except that he has a big heart and a desire to get a grip on himself and get better. And after some deep trouble, he does. He sorts out his relationship with his missing mother, gets the medication he needs, and learns how to stay on task in school.

In *Joey Pigza Loses Control* Joey seeks a relationship with his absent father – a man who, like Joey, is hyperactive but a lot bigger. Carter Pigza says Joey doesn't need medication to control his impulsive behaviour – just old-fashioned 'self-control'. He flushes Joey's medication down the toilet and leaves Joey to slowly, and knowingly, lose control of himself until he can work his way back to his mother.

And now, in *What Would Joey Do?*, Joey decides that he can help the adults in his life, who seem unable to solve their own problems. He becomes 'Mr Helpful' and is determined through his positive attitude and unrelenting efforts to mop up all the messy corners of his life.

In the United States, 'W.W.J.D.?' stands for 'What Would Jesus Do?' It is a popular question asked by fundamentalist Christians who are eager to make moral decisions based on what they think Jesus Christ might do under the same circumstances. Often these people wear 'W.W.J.D.?' jewellery, zipper pulls and T-shirts. Most often I see the saying on car bumper stickers and on roadside billboards. Many people ask themselves this question quite seriously – like Joey's new home-school teacher Mrs Lapp, who asks Joey the question every morning. And as Joey tries to imagine what Jesus might do around his house, with his parents, with his life, he knows that ultimately he must find the right answers on his own. In *What Would Joey Do?* Joey Pigza faces his biggest challenge yet – solving problems for people who are not looking for answers.

Jack Gantos

1.

sparks

About three weeks ago Dad suddenly showed up in town and started buzzing us on his motorcycle at all hours of the day and night. At first I was afraid because I thought he had come to get me, but I was wrong. He was much more interested in Mom. I lost track of how many times he roared down our street and ran the corner traffic light past Quips Pub, where Mom lounged in the leather window seat sipping a mixed drink with her new boyfriend while making plans for her future. Dad must have spotted her there during one of his rounds. He didn't say

7

anything, but he'd look at her in the window like she was something he wanted. Then, he'd blast off. It was dark out, I could look through my back bedroom window and between the lines of damp laundry catch his single jittery headlight brightly striking the white marble tombstones lined up like crooked teeth behind our yard as he cut through St Mary's Cemetery and raced out and around the neighbourhood making a crazy eight before he looped back down Plum Street and past our house again. He must have been watching her closely because sometimes he'd show up the minute she got home from work. Then, her face would go red and I'd watch her run out to the front porch and yell at him as he raced by, but the louder she yelled the louder he revved the engine.

'I'm losing my patience with that man,' Mom would say when she came back inside, pacing wildly up the hall, swinging around and down again, past the furniture and me and Pablo and Grandma, as if she too were on a motorcycle that was darting past us.

'If you didn't yell at him I bet he'd get bored and go home,' I said once while trying to be helpful.

'He'd better return to the hole he lives in,' she said, 'or I'll send him into the next kingdom.'

'Just ignore him,' I advised. 'It'll drive him nuts.'

'And I'll go nuts if I don't yell at him,' she replied.

I knew Dad. Yelling at him was only going to make him want to yell back twice as loud. The only way Mom could be louder than him was to be quiet. He couldn't stand to be ignored and Mom couldn't stand to be quiet, so I knew something bad was on the way. I could feel it coming, just as I could hear his motorcycle circling.

And then it finally happened. We were out on the front porch late one afternoon. I was squatted down behind a wooden railing, holding my dog Pablo and peeking out between the slats, while Mom was on the top step hollering at Dad. The silencer on his motorcycle was dragging across the asphalt and a steady stream of sparks trailed behind him like the lighted fuse on a bomb that was headed right at our house. He looked like a giant black bat in his studded leather biker outfit with his hands raised up in the air on

9

his chopper handlebars and his shiny blue-eyed wraparound sunglasses clamped tight against his bony face. He had already circled our block about ten times in a row and each time he got a little closer to the house, as if he were zeroing in on a target. He was really flying and when he reached our yard he jerked up on his handlebars and lifted his front wheel over the stone kerb. When his back wheel hit the kerb the rear of the chopper bounced up and almost catapulted him forward. Still, he hung on and landed with a smack back in his seat as he fishtailed across the sidewalk and headed straight for the porch.

But Mom was waiting for him, and she was ready for a fight. As soon as he jumped the kerb she sprang forward and bolted down the porch stairs with a broom held up over her head as if she would swat him like a biker vampire who had come to suck our blood. But when she reached the bottom stair and leaped forward he stuck out his leg with a huge, nasty boot on the end of it and without flinching knocked her back on her butt as he turned and roared across our rutted dirt yard and towards the street. She bounced just once and flattened out like something heavy dropped from the roof as he laughed, or cursed, or announced his return – I couldn't tell which because of the engine noise, and with Mom's yelling and Pablo's yapping in my ear. I couldn't hear anything clearly. Then, as he flew off the yard, his silencer hit the kerb and suddenly there was an explosion of sparks like a comet smashing into the earth, only it was his silencer flipping into the air and spinning like a pinwheel, showering the street with sparks. Instantly the engine noise was a hundred times louder and I had to drop Pablo to cover my ears as Dad snarled down to the end of the block where he turned right and I could hear him open the throttle along the straight and rattle the windows across the neighbourhood, across all of Lancaster, maybe the whole state of Pennsylvania.

And then Mom scrambled to her feet and raised her fist in the air. 'So you want to play dirty?' she hollered. '*I'll* show you what dirty is!' She charged up the porch stairs two at a time. 'Outta my way,' she panted, and rushed past me with her broom held forward like a witch about to launch herself.

'Are you OK?' I asked. 'Are you hurt?'

'This time I'm gonna kill that creep,' she

promised with a murderous look on her face that made her words seem real to me. 'I should've done it years ago and put him out of *my* misery.'

I followed her into the house.

'I don't think you should kill him,' I said, and held onto the back end of the broom. 'He's just a nut.'

'A dangerous pain-in-the-butt nut,' she replied, and yanked the broom away. 'He can't scare me, but I'm gonna make him pay for messing with you.'

'Don't do it because of me,' I said. 'Just leave him alone and he'll go away.'

'No, this time he has to *pay*.'

'But he doesn't owe me anything,' I pleaded. 'Just lock the door and call the police.'

'Hey, I'm doing this for you!' she replied, and gave me an exasperated look as if I didn't appreciate her protection.

'But you don't have to,' I said.

'Fine! Fine!' she snapped. 'Fine!'

And because it looked like she might blow a gasket I stood up on my tiptoes and imitated her by saying 'Fine! Fine!' right back, just like a mirror she might see herself in and calm down, and then we would call the cops and they would scare Dad away and all of this would be over with.

But my little act didn't work.

Instead, her eyes bugged out and she was definitely not calm. 'If you won't help just stay out of my way,' she said, glaring at me. Then she pointed to the carpet and gave me an intense, squinty look. 'Don't you dare move from this spot.' Her finger stabbed the air over the dark stain where Pablo had made a little doggy mess after we left him behind while we did our ten-mile walkathon against lung cancer that almost killed us. Her new boyfriend – who has a name that sounds like Tooth Decay but is really Booth Duprey – took us. He's very enthusiastic.

'I can't promise that I won't move,' I said. 'What if I have to scratch my nose or go to the bathroom or faint?'

She grabbed me by the neck of my shirt and yanked my face towards hers. 'Look into my eyes!' she demanded. 'Look! Can't you see I'm half nuts right now? That I'm at my wits' end and the last thing I need is you playing games with me?'

'Sorry,' I said in a tiny voice the size of a talking ant. 'Soooooo sorry.'

Then she let me go and ran out the back door hollering, 'You are a dead man, Carter Pigza!' She sprinted across the yard and out the metal gate and into the cemetery behind our house. She was going to ambush him from behind the big silver statue of Jesus, who had his arms stretched out from side to side like someone trying to stop a fight.

'What in the blazes is going on?' Grandma growled from her curtained-off corner of the living-room.

Grandma was living with us again. When I was little she took care of me. Then Mom returned and they bumped heads over how to raise me so Grandma moved in with Dad. But Dad drove his own mom crazy too. When she came back at the end of the summer there wasn't an empty bedroom for her, so Mom pushed the couch into a corner of the living room for a bed, then rigged up a plastic shower curtain that pulled to and fro and gave her a bit of privacy. But nothing gave us privacy from her.

I pulled the shower curtain to one side and covered my eyes. Sometimes she wasn't fully dressed, and with her clothes off and teeth out it was like lifting the lid on a coffin.

But she was sitting up with a cutting board across her lap that she used as a desk. She had taken a job earning money at home by folding junk-mail advertisements and stuffing them into envelopes. She had a lot of paper cuts on her tongue which only made her meaner.

'I said, what in the blazes is going on out there? You bring home a jackhammer?' She started coughing so loudly I didn't think she could hear me reply that Dad was buzzing us again and mom had snapped and was running with a broom from the front yard to the cemetery.

But Grandma had heard everything I said, and once she sucked a few deep breaths out of the tube from her oxygen tank, she swelled up and blurted out, 'This is exactly how it was before you were hatched. Always flirtin'. Always this kind of fightin' back and forth so that you never knew if he wanted to kiss her or kill her, and she is just dumb enough to play his little dating game. I've seen this before when he left her pregnant, then returned and made up, and then they had a big blowout and you were born, and the next thing you know he swings by and she runs

15

off with him and leaves you to me. I didn't see much of her until she walked in the door last year and started treating me like an old shoe.'

'She's not interested in Dad. She already has Booth,' I said. 'They're in *love.*'

Grandma's laugh sounded like flames crackling. 'Not for long,' she predicted. 'Once he gets wind of these antics he'll pack up his heart and be long gone and hard to find.'

In the distance I could hear Dad slow down in order to slip through the narrow back gate in the cemetery fence, and I knew he had one more short straight before he'd reach the corner of our street and would soon be ripping past our house and I didn't want to miss him. 'Relax,' I said to Grandma.

'Relax?' she said. 'Impossible. I'm back here because when you left me at your father's I knew I had made a big mistake leaving you in the first place. Oh no, I won't relax until I'm running this show again.'

Suddenly Mom staggered through the back door. She bent over with her hands on her knees and took a few deep breaths. 'Darn it,' she growled, then stood up. 'I missed him and he kicked me on my can again.' Once she got her breath back she ran out the front door and squatted down behind the busted porch swing that was hanging lopsided from me dancing on it until the chain on one end pulled out of the ceiling.

'Don't you have anything else to do besides sit around here and watch this catfight?' Grandma asked.

'Not right now,' I said.

'Then come here,' she whispered. I leaned forward and she reached out and grabbed my ears as she hoisted herself from the couch with a grunt.

'Ouch,' I cried. Her old bony fingers were like monkey claws.

'Don't you have some friends you need to visit?'

'No,' I said, and wrestled away from her. I wanted to get to the front porch. I hadn't seen my parents together very much and I had missed all their fireworks. Every other kid gets to see their parents fight, so watching mine actually made me feel kind of normal.

'You know, Joey,' Grandma said, 'you gotta make some friends.'

'I have Pablo,' I said.

'Pablo is a dog,' she replied.

'He's more than a dog,' I cut in. 'When I

rub his belly a genie pops out his mouth and grants me wishes.'

'I don't care if he does card tricks, he's still a dog,' she shot back. 'Just a dog. Face it. Nothing but a dog – and not much of one at that. So don't tell me what he is or isn't. What you need is a person friend your own age. Not a genie, or a wind-up toy, or a robot. Pablo should go play with other dogs and you should go make a friend.'

'I almost have a friend,' I said.

'Who?' she spit back. 'That mean blind girl who makes you cry?'

I never should have told Grandma that Olivia Lapp made me cry.

'She hates you,' Grandma continued. 'You said so yourself.'

'Well, I'm working on her,' I said. 'You'll see.'

'Yeah,' Grandma scoffed, 'I'll believe it when I see it.'

Just then I heard Dad downshift, turn the corner, and start tearing up our street.

'Excuse me,' I said to Grandma and skipped away. 'I don't want to miss this.'

I reached the porch just as Dad was making his first move. He launched his chopper up over the kerb as Mom dashed down the stairs with the broom held out like a bayonet. When he saw her he smiled and stuck out his boot again, but this time she thrust the handle towards his front wheel. There was a snapping sound as the handle jammed into the spokes and the bike flipped through the air. Dad shot forward yowling like a cat blasted out of a cannon. Where our yard stopped and the neighbour's began stood a dead apple tree with grey branches sticking out like dry old bolts of lightning, and he went sprawling into it and something cracked and then he just hung there with his legs kicking as the tree vibrated.

The motorcycle tumbled head-over-heels behind him, hit the trunk of the tree, and choked to a stop. Suddenly it was very quiet. Then Dad cried out, 'Help me, I'm speared on a branch!'

And Mom screamed. 'Oh my God, I killed him!'

'He's not dead yet,' I said. 'He's still talking.'

'Who's dead?' Grandma asked as she shuffled onto the porch, then broke into a phlegmy cough. Every time she spoke it sounded like me sucking milk spit through a straw.

'Dad,' I blurted out. 'He's stuck on a tree branch, but he's alive.'

'Unless that branch pierced his heart he'll be fine,' she said. 'He's part vampire.'

'That's just what I thought,' I said.

'Well, it's about time you realize we are alike,' she confirmed. 'You and me, we're cut from the same cloth. Now run inside and call an ambulance before his howling attracts every cat in the neighbourhood.'

I ran inside for the phone and tried to dial 911 but I was so worked up I couldn't get the numbers right and I kept jabbing at the dial like a hyper woodpecker until by luck I got directory assistance and I just told the lady to give me 911. When the emergency operator answered I was breathing as hard as Grandma. 'We've had a motorcycle accident,' I said. 'Send an ambulance.' I fired out the address, then hung up and ran back to the porch.

'Hang on, Dad!' I yelled. 'I called the ambulance.' Just then the branch snapped and he fell to the ground like a rotten apple. He moaned loudly, and I could see a piece of bloody branch sticking through a gap between his leather jacket and his pants.

Mom knelt down beside him with one hand on his head and the other on the branch that came out of his back around the outside of his ribs. 'Don't worry,' she said. 'Don't worry. It's just a little branch. It won't kill you.'

It wasn't killing him, but he was bleeding, and complaining and squirming around like when you step on a snake. 'Dang it, I'm going to have the cops put you in jail for attempted murder.'

'Quiet,' she said. 'Just relax.'

'You'll spend the rest of your life in prison,' he threatened. Then he let out a desperate yowl because at that moment Mom grabbed the piece of branch and gave it a good shake.

'I said be quiet,' she growled. 'And don't threaten me or else you won't be around to see the police arrest you for assault. What I did was self-defence.'

If he was dying, he was doing it loudly. 'You always wanted to kill me and now you have. I was just trying to have a little fun and as usual you have to go and ruin it.'

'Shut up, you big baby,' she said, and wiggled the branch as if she were shifting gears.

'Owww,' he moaned. 'Don't hurt me.'

'What's it matter now that you're dying?'

I started to run towards them but Grandma snatched my shirt from behind. 'Joey, you stay up here on the porch and leave those two fools alone.'

'But I want to help,' I pleaded.

'You can't,' she replied. 'They don't want help. They're just gluttons for punishment. Either they're givin' a beating or gettin' one.'

I must have figured she was right because I stopped in my tracks and stayed by her side. She jerked me around behind her as if she were protecting me from a fire. 'Listen,' she said. 'I can hear a siren.'

And in a minute an ambulance pulled up and a couple of paramedics jumped out and ran over to Dad. One of them slowly started to feel his arms and legs for broken bones while the other one took a pair of shears and cut his jacket so he could look at the branch. 'Just relax, mister,' he kept saying. 'It's not as bad as it looks. Just calm down and breathe normal.'

'Hell's bells,' Dad replied. 'How can I calm down when I have a piece of tree running through my body and you've cut up my leathers?'

'It's just a flesh wound,' the medic said. 'It's only gone through the fat on the outside of your ribs.'

'I'm dying,' he said. 'I'm bleeding to death.'

'Settle down,' the medic said, 'and you won't bleed as much.'

'He can't settle down,' Mom said. 'He's permanently jerky.'

Dad started to say something but the other medic put a big foam collar around his neck that pushed his chin up so he couldn't talk any more. Then they shifted him sideways onto a wooden stretcher and I could see right away that even though he was slick with blood the piece of branch that was poking through him was only about as big around as a cue stick.

Mom climbed into the ambulance with him, and just before the driver closed the door I could see her reach for Dad's hand and hold it tight.

Grandma saw it too. 'What'd I tell you,' she said bitterly after they sped off. 'They're a couple of sick love-puppies who deserve each other.'

As soon as the ambulance was out of sight, a police car slowly rolled up to our house and two cops got out. One of them had a clip-board and the other one had a walkie-talkie that squawked like an angry parrot trapped in a box. I knew I should have been upset about what had happened, really off the wall and pulling my hair out in clumps, but somehow I wasn't. I just stood there and breathed as deeply as I could and then let all the air leak out until I felt empty inside, as if my breath were a visitor who entered me, looked around, found nothing of special interest, and left.

Grandma turned and stared down at me with a harsh look on her lined face. 'Go get lost,' she said, wheezing like a broken accordion.

'What are you going to tell them?' I asked.

'Nothing,' Grandma replied, and reached down the back of my shirt and peeled off my med patch that kept me from being too hyper. Sometimes we shared medication. The doctor wouldn't give her a patch for being hyper, because he said at her age hyper was good. 'Let me borrow this for a few minutes while the cops are here,' she said, and slapped it on the side of her neck as if she were covering up a vampire bite.

'Why can't I stay and tell them what I saw?'

'Because you might tell the truth, and as far as I'm concerned, who can say between the two of those nuts which one is criminally insane and which one is mentally ill? Let the cops figure it out on their own. Now, skedaddle.'

'OK,' I said, and shrugged. 'See you later.' Then I scooped Pablo up, grabbed the leash that was hanging over the doorknob, and zipped out the back door.

2.

PEEK-a-Boo!

When I left the house that evening, I speed-walked with my arms swinging back and forth and half dragged and half yanked poor Pablo down to the hospital emergency room to see if there was anything I could do to help. Even though Pablo's little pink tongue was hanging out from exhaustion and he couldn't walk another step even if he wanted, I still tied him to the fence, then went inside and asked a nurse about Dad. She set her lips so tightly together they looked like a line of red wire. It was a look I was used to seeing and I knew she was trying to decide something. Then finally she told me he had run off.

'Did you see which way he went?' I asked.

'No,' she replied. 'The doctor tried to keep him overnight for observation after he stitched him up, but your dad sneaked out the fire exit. We have some antibiotics for him to take, so if you see him, have him return for them. OK?'

'Can I give him the medicine?' I asked, and held out my hand. I figured he was still angry with me for running back to Mom this summer after he flipped out during our first visit ever, and I thought if I had some medicine for him, he would calm down and know I really wanted to help him get better. I didn't want him to be mad at me for ever, so it was only fair that I shouldn't be mad at him now. But I did have to be careful. He had already proved he was more than I could handle.

'No,' she said. 'He has to get it himself.'

'He won't do that,' I said.

'Then your mom can get it for him.'

'She definitely won't,' I said. 'And my grandma won't do it either because she hardly leaves the couch any more. Believe me, I'm the only one who can help.'

'Well, I'm sorry,' she said. 'But we don't give medicine to minors. Do you understand what . . . I . . . am . . . say . . . ing?' She spoke the last part so slowly it confused me and then I guessed that when my parents had stopped holding hands they had started acting badly again, and now the nurse thought I was abused or deranged in some way from being around them.

'Can I ask you a question?' I asked.

She nodded.

'Do my parents seem unusual to you? Because they seem a little unusual to me.'

'Do your parents call each other bad names at home?' the nurse asked, bending down to look me straight in the eyes.

'They call each other bad names *anywhere*,' I replied. 'My grandmother thinks they are criminally insane.'

'Do you want to talk with someone at the hospital about this?' she asked, dropping down on both knees and reaching for my hands with hers. When she realized she still had on her white rubber gloves she began to peel them off, which made a noise like a duck being strangled.

'I have to go,' I said suddenly, backing away. 'Thanks for your help.' I turned and ran and was just out the door when it hit me that Dad had run away from her too, and now I was pulling the same stunt he did. She must have thought we were both nuts, and that it was true what they say – the apple doesn't fall far from the tree. And as if that weren't bad enough, as soon as I untied Pablo I began to think that maybe something really awful had happened in the hospital and maybe Mom was hurt and that's why Dad ran away, and the nurse was just trying to break the news to me. That stopped me in my tracks, but before my old nervous habit of pulling my own hair out got my hands going, I saw a pay phone. I dug into my pocket and fished out some change and called home to make sure she was OK. Mom answered and before I could get some words out she hollered. 'Hello? Hello?' She was spittin' mad, and in the background I heard pots and pans banging together, and suddenly I remembered Booth was coming for dinner and Mom was cooking. Then she yelled, 'Carter Pigza, if this is you, I swear I will call the phone company and tell them you are harassing me. You *pig*!'

After that it was too hard to say the words that it was just her kid on the other end calling to hear her nice Mom voice so I would know she was OK. So I gently hung up the phone and quickly walked home because I didn't want to be late and ruin Mom's dinner plans, or her future plans with Booth, which she said looked 'promising'. But before I walked into the house, I stood and stared at the tree Dad had got hung up on. Then I squatted down and patted the dark ground with my open hand. I don't know why I wanted to feel where his blood had made the dirt all sticky, but as I patted the spot I felt sorry for him, as if my touch could make his cut feel better. I always wanted him to be a good dad, but since he wasn't, I just wanted him to be a good person. When I stood up, I examined his motorcycle. The fenders were scratched and dented, but the rest of it looked OK. Then I glanced over my shoulder and saw the silencer in the street. It looked like a saxophone that a ten-ton truck had run over, and I picked it up and carried it into the house and hid it in my room before anyone noticed I had returned. Then I went to the bathroom and scrubbed the sticky dirt and black silencer soot off my hands until the sink was filthy, and I had to clean that too because Mom was having me help out more around the house since she worked longer hours and Grandma could no longer clean up after herself. Just thinking about how sick she was made me feel fizzy inside, so I opened the cabinet and got out a new med patch. I peeled off the back and stuck it to my shoulder.

When I first met Booth after I returned from spending the summer at Dad's house, he tried to be friendly to me. I had heard Mom angrily tell him about Dad being a nut and me running away from him, and I knew Booth wanted to help smooth it all out by listening and just being a good guy. I liked that about him – the madder Mom got, the calmer Booth became. Still, he was another guy in the house, and Mom was mine first, and her being my mom is a thousand times more important than her being some guy's girlfriend. So even though Booth wasn't trying to run the show, he was still in the way.

Mom had taken on extra work styling

brides' hair at a place called Mimi's Wedding World, and that's where she met Booth, who was the chief photographer. They had been going out secretly before Mom introduced him to me. She must have told him I was 'wired' because before long, he wanted to get me involved in what he called some 'upbeat group activities'. The next thing I knew I was enrolled in the Southern Praying Mantis Federation Karate Club, run by a man named Sifu Sam. At first I thought it would be fun to get all dressed up in a karate outfit and learn how to kick-box and chop people in half with a single *whack* as if my hand were a deadly meat cleaver. But what happened was the complete opposite. We learned in slow motion how to do a dozen different moves that were important to how a praying mantis defends itself. The whole time I felt like a bug stuck in honey, and I really couldn't keep my mind on being still, because every time Booth drove me, he wanted to talk about Mom and about getting married to her and about being a *super* dad to me and starting over. So all during my lesson in slow motion, my brain was racing on about my uncomfortable car ride with him and sometimes I'd forget about what I was doing and fall over onto my back with my insect legs and arms wiggling up in the air as if a giant shoe were about to crush me.

Even though I didn't want to be a praying mantis, I did like the idea of being good at karate, so at home I'd put on Mom's white terrycloth bathrobe and run out to my backyard and begin to hop and spin in mid-air and karate-chop everything I could find. One day I hacked at the wooden birdhouse that was built like a lolly-stick log cabin and with one swing of my hand I crushed the roof. That was a good start. Then I clanged my knuckles off the metal clothesline pole but when I looked really closely at the spot where I hit the pole I couldn't find a dent even though my hand was still vibrating. Afterwards I tried to crack in half an old marble tombstone Dad had stolen out of the cemetery and brought home because it had his name on it already – CARTER PIGZA 1847–1904. I really hurt the fleshy side of my hand and it turned purple and I had to ice it down and have it wrapped in an Ace bandage for a week, which made Mom ask me day in and day out if I needed to increase my meds. After that the karate idea sort of faded away. And my talks with Booth did too.

Next he tried to get along with Grandma, but that was a mistake. One night he asked if she wanted to go to the senior citizens' centre for a bingo tournament, and she told him she'd rather visit the morgue and hang out with the real dead people than go to the senior citizens' centre and hang out with the living dead.

'Aw, come on,' Booth crooned, and reached for her elbow. 'You don't really mean that.'

'Mister,' she said, jerking away and sizing him up with a knitting needle as if she were going to pin him to the wall, 'I don't say *anything* unless I mean it.'

Booth smiled and slipped his hands into his pockets, and I could tell in his mind he knew we were not an ordinary family and he had his work cut out for himself if he was going to win us over. I also knew he had just better stick with winning over Mom, because Grandma and I didn't pay him much attention and never would. It's not that we didn't like him, but he was just one more person to listen to, and in our house, which was a lot like those family TV talk shows where everyone yells at once, we didn't need another opinion.

When I came out of the bathroom from washing the silencer dirt off my hands, the sink, and the floor, I went into the living room. Booth was already sitting in a chair with his legs neatly crossed and a little silver camera in his lap. He had arrived from work with all his photographic equipment, and as soon as he saw me, he snapped my picture and started talking right away about how lucky he was to have a job taking pictures of people on the happiest day of their lives, and that weddings had to be the most glorious event on earth, and that he couldn't wait to get married someday so he could make a video of it like a Hollywood movie with a hundred camera angles and close-ups and harps playing in the background, and children dressed like golden angels, with pink cupids shooting rubber love arrows – and he kept talking, but by then Grandma had rolled her bloodshot eyes more times than a losing slot machine and was shuffling her way towards the sofa to hide behind her curtain and smoke a cigarette. I edged my way across the floor until I was behind the upright lamp and could peek around the fringed shade at Mom just to see her expression every time he mentioned marriage. Whatever she was thinking, she didn't show it. Her face looked like a picture of someone trying to solve a crossword puzzle. But not having an audience didn't trouble Booth and he went from talking to whistling like a gooney bird while fooling with his camera.

'You know why I like Booth?' Mom had said to me one night. She was tapping sand out of my sneakers into the palm of her hand.

'Why?' I asked. I wasn't really listening because I was trying to fix an old waffle maker I had found in the big Goodwill donation bin up the street. The wires were frayed and I was taping them together and getting ready to plug them in.

'Because he is so upbeat. Nothing gets him down. He can always find the silver lining in a bad situation.'

'He must be good at it,' I replied, 'because he sure seems to like it around here.'

'That's because I'm the silver lining,' she chirped. 'and you could improve your attitude and learn a thing or two from him.' She tossed my shoes into the closet and brushed the sand from her hands on the back of her pants. 'He makes me feel like we have a real chance at a normal family life. What do you think of that?'

I didn't know what to say because I didn't know anything about normal family life. I just leaned forward and plugged in my waffle maker and something down the hallway went *pop!* Then the lights went out.

'You blew a fuse,' Mom said.

'Sorry,' I whispered, but I wasn't worried. I had blown and changed fuses before. My all-time list of objects stuck in sockets included a thermometer, a fork, a knitting needle, a penknife, an ice pick, a wet Q-tip, tweezers, and a pair of Mom's flea market earrings that got smoking hot and melted like metal tears.

Tonight since Booth was present, Mom insisted that we all sit down at the dining-room table together and not eat in front of the TV like everyone wanted. So when Booth stopped talking about weddings, and when

Grandma finished her cigarette, and when I finished spying on Mom's face, we all took our places, which meant I sat next to Booth because Mom was still trying to fix us up. She had cooked spaghetti and put the platter down in the middle of the table. She served us all, and silently we began to eat. I looked at my watch. Seven seconds passed before Booth couldn't hold himself back any longer.

'Fran, this is the best spaghetti I've ever eaten,' he announced. 'You must be part Italian.'

Mom giggled.

Grandma looked at me and frowned so forcefully her mouth bent down like a horseshoe.

'And, Granny Pigza,' he said like a game-show host about to hand her the keys to a new car, 'how was your day?'

'Just another hurdle on my way to the grave,' she said matter-of-factly.

Booth gave a little chuckle. 'You are a straight shooter,' he said. 'Anyone who can speak the unvarnished truth is to be admired.' He lifted his camera to take her picture. 'Give me a little smile,' he said. She pushed out her lower dentures like a horse spitting its bit.

Then he turned his search for a silver lining towards me. 'How's the new home-school going, buddy?'

My head was someplace else. It had already been a tough day and I was feeling pretty drifty when I remembered I had forgotten to check on my yard-gnome friends on the way home from the hospital. There's a house down the street with a group of those little gnomes – the kind with white beards and red and green outfits and matching caps – and I always wonder what they are up to. Sometimes they are balanced on ceramic toadstools. Sometimes they are peeking out from under bushes, or leaning against huge spotted frogs. I wonder when nobody's looking if they run over and kick those big blue and green mirrored balls in other yards and chase the pigeons around and try to capture squirrels for a barbecue and dig holes and build traps for the dogs that come into their yard and lift their leg on them? They've sort of become my friends, and I took the new plastic label gun that Grandma had got me with her cigarette coupons and made up names for all of them and stuck them to the backs of their heads. There is IGOR I HATE YOU because he carries a little hatchet and looks evil, and LEG-LIFT HANS because he is Pablo's favourite, and the HUNCHBACK OF PLUM STREET because he has a nasty hunch and a lazy eye, and the one who is missing most of his face I named I'M DOPEY – HIT ME AGAIN after one of the seven dwarfs, because he was always my favourite.

I make up conversations they might all have if they came to life and wanted something real to do besides being posed like goofballs all day long. In a way I felt a lot like those gnomes because they aren't used for much more than a decoration, and since coming back from spending time at my dad's house in Pittsburgh that's how I felt once Mom told me she had a new boyfriend and she wanted me to be the best Joey I could be, which to me meant 'Don't do any weird Joey stuff' that would scare her boyfriend off. Not that I'm weird, but sometimes I don't think she understands that there is a difference between the stuff I want to do and the stuff I do just because I let myself go, like when you let the air out of a balloon and it goes swooping around full of silliness like a butterfly hugging itself. Because every time I get an idea about something and tell her about it she treats me like the old wired Joey and she replies, 'Did you think that through all the way?' And even though I want to unscrew my head and bounce it wickedly off the walls and scream at the top of my lungs, 'Can I get back to you on that?' I don't. Instead I look her directly in the eyes and relax my shoulders and stretch out my fingers and give a pretend little Pablo yawn, and when I can see her face swelling as if she's about to erupt, I reply, 'Yes, Mom, I thought it all the way through. All the way, from the beginning to the end, and I considered every particle in between.' This works OK if I'm doing something like using white glue to make a kite out of the chopsticks and paper menu that always come with the Chinese takeout food. But if I'm just totally spacing out and doing anything that pops into my mind, like trying to screw my shoes to the bedroom wall as if they've come alive and are walking up the sides and on the ceiling and on the furniture, she pitches a fit and tells me I'm not thinking things through and that to a normal person I look a bit 'out of the ordinary'. That's her new way of describing me to Booth. She won't call me anything like *strange* or *abnormal* or *peculiar*. She just says things like, 'Oh, don't mind that Joey is trying to get pet termites to live in the woodwork. He's not like other boys. He is out of the ordinary.' And Booth, whose head is so rectangular it looks like a shoe box with a nose stuck on one long side, gives me that I-didn't-raise-you-to-be-this-way-but-I'll-put-up-with-you-as-long-as-your-mom-is-my-girlfriend-otherwise-I-would-put-you-in-a-rubber-room look. In return I give him my Don't-fall-asleep-on-the-couch-because-when-you-wake-up-you-might-find-that-I-slowly-cut-all-your-clothes-off-and-when-you-stand-you-will-be-totally-naked-and-Grandma-and-I-will-have-your-camera-ha-ha-ha look.

I was just thinking of making an I'M WITH STUPID label and sticking it to my forehead when Mom said sharply, 'Joey! Booth asked you a question.'

'Huh?' I said.

'*Huh* is not a word,' Mom corrected.

'How's the home-schooling?' Booth asked, starting at square one again.

'Fine, I guess,' I said to him.

'Joey's so smart,' Mom said, 'I'm thinking of starting a college fund for him. I saw an ad in the paper where the hospital is doing a study on active boys, and they'll pay if all he does is show up and go through a few tests every month. I thought maybe with that money we could start a little college savings account. A few dollars a month, and someday he'll be making millions and take care of me.'

Then before I could ask Mom what she meant about a hospital study, her face went all hard and she bolted straight up as if she were possessed by some demon. And in an instant she grabbed her water glass and whipped it as hard as she could across the table, over Booth's flat head, and through the dining-room window, which smashed into a thousand pieces.

'That son-of-a-gun!' she hollered.

'What the heck was that?' Grandma squawked. Mom didn't answer. By then she had jumped up and run to the window and stuck her head through the empty frame, which was edged with glass shards. She looked like a lion tamer with her head in the lion's mouth. 'Carter Pigza!' she yelled. 'Next time you peek through a window in this house you better expect a kitchen knife right between your eyes!'

'How about a kiss?' he hollered back. Then I could hear him belly laughing like a crazy gnome as he ran off, and a few moments later I heard the motorcycle start up, then die out.

'When I get my hands on you, I'll squeeze your neck until your head pops. You hear me?' Mom yelled.

I don't know if Dad heard her, but I'm sure the entire neighbourhood did. Then the motorcycle started again and caught, and he roared down Plum Street.

'Told you those two are lovebirds,' Grandma said to me.

Then we both looked over at Booth. His lips were sucked entirely inside his mouth so that it looked like a sock rolled inside out. He sat there as stiff as a stump not knowing what to do. And what could he do? Get up and run for his life? Get up and fix the window? Get up and help Mom catch Dad?

'Just roll with the punches,' Grandma advised him. 'You always have to consider that you're in the house of Pigza, where anything goes.'

He put on one of his fake smiles, which seemed to have lost its silver lining, and sat there stunned with his knife and fork quivering in each red fist until Mom came back and plopped down in her chair, and then he calmly asked, 'Fran, what was that all about?'

'He was peeking in the window,' Mom said furiously, pointing toward the smashed glass. 'He was spying on us, the little sneak, so I let him have it. I don't think he'll ever do that again.'

'This is just a suggestion,' he said delicately, 'but do you think you should call the police and lodge a complaint?'

'No,' she shot back. 'No. I can take care of him on my own.'

'OK,' Booth said. 'I was just offering a suggestion.' Then he reached across the table and picked up the platter of spaghetti and helped himself. 'This is real good,' he said in his upbeat voice. 'Probably the best I've ever eaten.'

'Oh, for Pete's sake,' Mom said harshly. 'It's just *spaghetti*. You boil the noodles, and you toss a jar of sauce on it.' Then she stood up and marched down the hall and into her room. I heard a drawer open, then slam, and when she marched back to the table, she had on fresh lipstick and was carrying a handbag. She looked at us. We looked back at her. 'I don't know why,' she said angrily, 'but when your dad is around I always seem to sink to his level.'

She stuck out her elbow as if it were the handle on a teapot. 'Come on, Booth,' she said. 'Let's go have a cocktail and forget about this nonsense.'

'Sure,' he replied. 'Anything you say, Fran.' When he stood up, his little camera fell from his lap.

'Your camera,' I said politely, pointing towards the floor where Pablo was sniffing it.

'Come *on*,' Mom said more forcefully. Then, just as he grabbed the camera strap, Mom yanked him by the hand and just about jerked him out of his shoes. He stumbled forward and I don't think he fully caught his balance until he was out the door and down the steps and standing in the middle of the road saying, 'Whoa, boy.' I could see right away why Mom liked him. She was the boss.

Once their voices faded down the street, I began to clear the table. 'Do you think,' I said to Grandma as I stacked the plates, 'that I ought to follow them down to Quips and see if Mom is OK?'

'Joey,' Grandma said, 'you need a life. Leave these people alone, and think about yourself.'

'But it makes my happy when I keep an eye on her.'

'You know, Joey,' she said, 'let me give you some old lady advice. It's been my observation that those people who try to make everyone really, really happy are really the most miserable people of all.'

'I'm not miserable,' I said. 'I'm really happy. See.' And I ran up to her and smiled right in her face.

Grandma shoved my face away with her hand and got all huffy. 'You're bugging me,' she said. 'Go to bed.' Then she shuffled over to her couch, jerked her curtain closed, and turned on her oxygen tank. I could hear it hissing as she sucked on the tube.

'I'm just going to do the dishes,' I called in her direction. 'It will make Mom happy to come home to a clean kitchen.'

'Forget the dishes,' Grandma said. 'Go have some fun. What do you think she's doing?'

I really wasn't sure what Mom was doing. But whatever it was, I wanted her to be happy. After I finished the dishes and put the food away I swept up the glass spikes that had fallen inside the house, then went out back and took the plastic tablecloth off the picnic table. I wiped the dirt away with a wet sponge, got some thumbtacks, and pinned it up over the hole in the window.

After I brushed my teeth and washed up, I noticed Grandma's lamp was still on. I could see her shadow against the shower curtain. She was lying down with her head thrown back on the arm of the couch. The cigarette in her mouth looked like the last smoking tree after a forest fire.

'Go to sleep,' I said, 'before all your envelopes catch on fire and you burn the house down.'

'If I go to sleep, I might never wake up,' she replied. 'And I can't die, or everything around here will go to hell before I'm cold and in the grave.'

'Don't talk that way,' I said.

'You know why I'm still alive?' she said to me, exhaling like a punctured tyre.

''Cause you don't want to die?' I guessed.

She slowly pulled aside the curtain so that just her old turtle head stuck out. 'No. I do want to die. I'm *begging* to be put out of my misery. I just want to make sure you're in good shape before I check out. I took care of you in the beginning when you were a handful, but now that you've pulled yourself together . . .' She coughed, then took another drag. 'You got to get away from these people. You can't depend on people who can't run their own lives to tell you what to do. You got to make your own life. Once I see to it that you are headed in the right direction, then my job'll be done, and I can smoke cigars, drink hard liquor, and dance with the devil in style.'

'Grandma,' I said quietly, 'please don't talk that way. You scare me.'

'And here's another thing,' she continued. 'I've got a little letter-stuffing money set aside, as I've been saving for a lung replacement I'll never get. When I'm gone, you get to it first, you hear? Don't you go becoming no experiment at a hospital.'

'I hear you,' I said, even though I didn't want to.

She pointed her cigarette at the cigar box on the couch. 'There's an envelope in there. You take the money and spend it on yourself. Don't give a nickel to them. Because even after I'm dead, they'll be fussin' and fightin' over what's left of me.'

'You're not going to die,' I said. 'Stop it.'

'Yes, I am,' she replied. 'And soon too, so get used to the idea. And if you want me to die happy, you'd better stop trying to help your parents and join the real world, which is on the *outside* of this house.'

'I know,' I said. 'I know.'

'And you *have* to make a friend.'

'OK,' I said. 'OK. But I don't want to kill you if I ever do make one.'

'Joey, you're killing yourself if you don't make friends. You got to move on. I do too. As for the nuts, they'll do what they please.'

'Oh, stop talking that way,' I said. 'You're too old to talk that way.'

'I'm old enough to have seen everything

there is to see around here twice over, and I don't like what I see coming the third time around.'

'What do you see?' I asked. 'Tell me.'

'I'm not telling,' she said. 'But stick around, and you'll find out soon enough. Goodnight.' And she pulled the curtain back in place.

Brat Girl

3

When Mom came home that night, she slipped into my room and kissed me. I was asleep, but I knew she had done it because the next day there was a red kiss print stamped on my forehead. I saw it in the mirror when I went to the bathroom to change my patch, and it made me smile really big because I looked like a love letter about to be sent. Then I ran into Mom's room and she was still sleeping but I kissed her anyway and she half woke up and hugged me and pulled on my big ears and yanked my nose and kissed me some more. I *love* that feeling when my mom loves only *me, me, me*! But then, as I left her room, my smile twisted up like a rusty old nail when I remembered what I had to do next.

After I fixed Grandma and myself some breakfast, checked her oxygen tank level, fed Pablo, watered the plants, took out the trash, picked the stuck roaches out of the Roach Motels, and dialled the Dial-a-Joke number and got my one free laugh, I did what I didn't want to do every weekday morning. I stuffed Pablo into the top of my giant backpack and trudged over to Olivia Lapp's house to get my daily dose of abuse. My mother knew her mother, and one day they got to talking. That's how all this home-schooling business started. Mom was doing Mrs Lapp's hair one afternoon and they started comparing notes about their kids and about how best to raise them and before I knew it Mom came rushing home and said she had something 'life changing' to tell me.

'What?' I asked, thinking right away that it must be a big treat if it was going to change my life. I closed my eyes and spread my arms out as wide as I could so that even if she was giving me a giant experimental

Chihuahua – like a Chihuahua the size of a Great Dane – I could hold it in my arms.

'I'm putting you into a home-schooling situation,' she said.

I opened my eyes and my arms slapped down against my sides like a bird who has given up and would just rather fall to earth than fly.

She was nodding so furiously I knew I couldn't disagree without her having a melt-down. She continued, 'I had the greatest conversation with an old school chum.' And then she went on and on about how good home-schooling was going to be for me.

'But I'm already in school,' I said. 'I already have a teacher and a desk and books. I already have *homework*.'

'Not after tomorrow,' she said. 'Home-schooling is so much better. Plus, you won't have any kids to tease you.'

'But they don't bother me now,' I said. 'Honest.'

'Of course they bother you,' she replied, not listening to me one bit. 'Believe me, Joey, you can do this home-school all day and you will learn so much more. And you will be with really good people. Decent people.

People who care about the *whole* Joey. Not just the *physical* Joey, but the *emotional* and *spiritual* Joey.'

I glanced over to the wall mirror to make certain there were not three of me. There was just one, and he was looking like a skinny, pale, wide-eyed, *freaked-out* Joey. 'Do you want to know what I think?' I asked.

'You don't know what to think yet,' she replied. 'You have to try it first before you know.'

'Well,' I said, 'I just don't think it's a good idea. Like, I can hardly do homework at home. It would be a disaster for me to do schoolwork at home too.'

'With that attitude, you'll make sure it doesn't work,' she said.

'Well, what if I stay home and Grandma home-schools me?'

'Your grandma only knows how to stuff envelopes, smoke, curse, and die slowly,' she said.

'Hey!' Grandma squawked from behind her curtain. 'I heard that!'

'Sorry,' Mom said, and put her hand over her mouth, but her eyes were smiling.

'That's OK,' Grandma replied, sounding a

little hurt. 'I'll just cheer myself up by smoking another cigarette as I kill myself stuffing these damn envelopes.'

'See,' Mom whispered, 'in one breath she taught you everything she knows.' Then she bent down and gave me a kiss. 'Come on, sweetie,' she said with her lips buzzing my ear, and kissed me again. 'Just follow my lead on this one. I have a very good feeling I'm right. And if you don't agree with me, then you can do what you want to do. OK?' And she kissed me again. 'I'm doing this for your own good.'

'OK.' I said, slipping out from under her arms. 'I'll give it a try.'

The next day Mom went with me to school and spoke with the principal and filled out some papers while I inched down to my class and put all my personal stuff in a shopping bag and told my teacher, Mrs Lucchina, that I was going to be home-schooled.

She looked worried. 'Is your mom going to be your teacher?' she asked.

'No,' I said sadly, 'she already taught me how to wash, cut, dye, and dry hair. We do it to my grandma all the time.'

Then she pulled herself together and by

the time she knelt down she had a you-can-do-it look on her face. 'Good luck,' she said, staring directly into my eyes like when the eye doctor shines his light in. 'We'll miss you. But try your best no matter what, and let me know if you need some extra help. OK?'

'OK,' I said to her as I looked into her smooth blonde hair and saw over her shoulder the whole classroom of kids whose names I had already memorized because I had planned on making each one my friend. 'I'll try.'

So I was thinking all this half-sad, half-mixed-up stuff and telling myself to keep my chin up as I headed toward Olivia's house – she's the home-school girl I'm paired up with. It didn't take me long after I started going to her house to realize the only reason Mrs Lapp had me around was to try and be a good influence on her totally bratty sight-challenged daughter. 'She can be a little ornery,' Mrs Lapp warned me, 'but she's got a pure heart. Your mom said you are a good kid, so you can be my secret helper by showing Olivia how even a kid with a big problem can be nice.'

I hated being called a 'kid with a big problem', but I did like being a 'secret helper'. It made me feel like a superhero out in the world with a mission to do good things for people. 'I'll try my best,' I said to Mrs Lapp. 'Honest.'

And I was trying. But being a secret helper superhero wasn't working too well. Olivia was totally blind and liked to call herself 'blind as a brat!' because she couldn't see to do anything nice. Still, she had twenty-twenty vision for getting me in trouble. The first day there was a nightmare. After Mrs Lapp introduced us in the kitchen she left the room so we could 'get to know one another'. As soon as she was gone Olivia said, 'I already know about you being a hyper retard.'

I didn't know what to say back, and even if I did I couldn't because my throat was closed up like when I ran into a clothesline while sneaking through yards at night. I needed a drink. I stood up and got a pitcher of lemonade off the counter, but when I carried it to the table Olivia tripped me with her cane. I spilled it all over my special home-schooling citizenship book, and there was nothing I could do but holler for Mrs Lapp, then tell her it wasn't my fault, while Olivia's already dark eyes grew darker and cloudy as if there were a storm brewing inside them.

'Just do your best,' Mrs Lapp whispered to me. 'Don't let her get to you.' Then she went out back and hung the soggy book over the fence to dry out.

That afternoon I was totally distracted by my label gun. I spelled out GENIUS STICK and stuck it on my pencil. I put LEFT on the rubber toe of one sneaker, and RIGHT on the other because sometimes I put them on so fast I got them reversed and walked around like a dork.

'I love my new Tweety Pie watch,' I said to Olivia while she read a book in braille. Her fingers moved across the page like a tarantula taking a stroll. 'Would you like to touch it?' Booth had given it to me. He had found it at a wedding reception, and when he fastened it around my wrist he said the picture of Tweety reminded him of me. I stuck JOEY 'TWEETY' PIGZA on the plastic band.

'Take it off for a minute,' she said.

'Sure,' I replied. Even though she couldn't see it I thought I should be polite.

As soon as it was in her hand she stood up and calmly made her way over to the microwave. 'Watch this,' she said mischievously. She tossed it into the microwave and turned it on high, working the buttons quickly. The microwave began to rattle like a machine gun. Wisps of smoke leaked out the vent, and I thought it was going to explode. When her mom came running in, Olivia pointed to where I was jumping around and blurted out, 'He did it! He did it!' I told Mrs Lapp I didn't, but all she said was, 'Now, Joey, we all know better than to put things in the microwave – especially something with metal on it.' Then she had to use a spatula to scrape my melted Tweety Bird off the bottom of the microwave. It looked like a fried egg with the pitted metal clasp on one edge.

I spelled MEAN BLIND GIRL on the label gun and sneaked up next to Olivia and stuck it to her cane.

'Excuse me for a minute,' she said, staring directly into the bright ceiling lights without blinking, 'I have to go to the ladies' room.'

A minute after she returned, her mother marched into the kitchen. 'Joey,' she said forcefully, 'follow me, please.' She directed me into the bathroom. My name was scrawled in big loopy Magic Marker handwriting all over the bathroom walls. 'Explain this please.'

'I didn't do this,' I said. 'Cross my heart and hope to die.'

'Never hope to die,' Mrs Lapp cautioned. 'Hope is one of God's greatest gifts to the world.' Then she returned me to the kitchen and made me write a list of all the things I hoped for, and she taped it to the little chalkboard she had on her teaching easel, and later we went over the whole list one by one.

'You hope Pablo learns to speak?' she asked. 'And for jelly and jam to be the same thing? And for people to be able to hold their breath long enough for the bus to arrive? Joey, don't you think you should hope that people never lie or cheat or steal?'

'I didn't think of that,' I said, and shrugged.

'Well,' she replied, 'that's why you are here, because instead of thinking about things that don't count, I'll teach you to think about things that do count.'

My first day was a long day. They were like a mother-daughter tag team. As soon as Olivia worked me over with her bratty tricks, her mother started in with her rules for making me a better person. During quiet time we sat in the kitchen with the lights turned low and listened to a Bible recording chanted by monks. I just wanted to go home, and once I did get home, I began to worry about the next day.

The job of being Mrs Lapp's secret helper started every morning as I stood on their front doormat and stared at a little green plaque screwed at eye level onto her front door. Painted in cursive yellow letters were the initials W.W.J.D.?, which I learned stands for 'What would Jesus do?' Olivia's mom is very nice and very religious, and every time she opens the door, she greets me by singing, 'What would Jesus do?' like that is a piece of a song the doorbell plays. The first time she did it, I thought it was a home-school pop-quiz, and I wasn't exactly sure what Jesus would do, because we didn't go to church too often, and what I knew about Jesus was from a little prayer book Grandma gave me that said Jesus loved children so much he died in order to help save them from the sins they were born with – which was a scary thought because Grandma said to me about a million times, 'Joey, you are your own worst enemy.' So maybe I was born with something extra bad inside me.

I guess my mind had wandered after I rang the doorbell that first day because Mrs Lapp suddenly touched me on the tip of my nose and when I looked up at her she repeated, 'What would Jesus do?'

'How would I know?' I said, puzzled. Then I blurted out, 'Wipe his feet?' And I wiped mine back and forth like I was rolling a log in water because Mom had always told me to start a new project by putting my best foot forward and I figured my best foot would have to be clean.

'Well, maybe he would do that,' she had said. Then after a pause she added brightly, 'Why, I bet he did always wipe his feet. I bet he used his manners. Why, I think you are very polite,' she sang, and patted me on the head. 'Olivia can really learn some friendship skills from you.'

Since that first morning I've told Mrs Lapp that Jesus would clean his room, say please and thank you, always respect his parents, never talk back, eat his vegetables, floss his teeth, help wash the dishes, and use soap when taking a bath. I was running out of things to say, to tell you the truth.

So there I was again, the morning after the motorcycle crash, breathing deeply in front of the Lapps' front door and wiping my feet and trying to think of something helpful to say, but I couldn't, so I knocked and hoped for the best. I figured something would blurt out of my mouth.

Mrs Lapp opened the door and smiled. 'Good morning, Joey,' she sang. 'Now what would Jesus do?'

'Well, Mrs Lapp, I'm not really sure today,' I said, just thinking out loud. 'I believe I'd like to have Jesus come to my door and look at my W.W.J.D.? sign, and when I opened the door, I'd ask him. "What would Joey do?" because right now I need some answers to some big questions.' As soon as I said it, I figured Mrs Lapp might take offence at the idea that Jesus might knock on my door so I could ask him a question. After all, he was supposed to be the most perfect person who ever lived, and I was like an encyclopaedia of imperfections, so there was no reason he would come to me. So I smiled my big smile that stretched my face from ear to ear and held it that way until I could feel my dry lips cracking.

'Oh,' she said, stepping back, 'that's an interesting thought. What would you ask him?'

'Well,' I said, and took a deep breath, 'my dad showed up on a motorcycle and my mom who claims not to like him stuck a broom in the spokes yesterday as he buzzed our front yard and he ended up flying through the air and stabbing himself on a tree branch, so then I thought she liked him again but it turns out she didn't because later she tried to hit him in the face with a glass in front of her new boyfriend. So I think I'd ask Jesus if I should try to help my parents get along, or if I should just ignore them and get on with my life like my grandmother says I should.'

'Now, honey,' Mrs Lapp said calmly, and touched her fingertips to her heart, 'Jesus taught us to always tell the truth.'

'I am telling the truth,' I insisted. 'My family is scaring me a little bit. I used to think they were normal, but now I'm thinking they are something *other* than normal.'

Mrs Lapp took a deep breath. 'God works in mysterious ways,' she said. 'Don't give up on your family. They are the way they are for a reason, even if you don't know it yet.'

'Well, I'd really like to know the reason,' I said, 'because I'm trying my best, but some days are pretty confusing.'

'Yes,' she said, and took a deep breath. 'Some days *are* confusing.' And I knew she meant Olivia was giving her a hard time and that God was being mysterious again.

I dragged my backpack with Pablo sleeping inside through the doorway. The little alarm chime went off like at a store just to announce someone was coming or going. I figured Mrs Lapp was always afraid Olivia might wander off on her own.

In the kitchen, where we spent most of our school day, I held my hands up over my eyes to keep from squinting. The ceiling was covered with overhead lights. They didn't help her see, but Mrs Lapp told me Olivia suffered from 'light deprivation syndrome' and the extra light she absorbed through her skin was good for her mood. It wasn't working today.

Olivia was sitting at the table with a halo-shaped cookie cutter hovering over a sheet of cookie dough as she stared down at it. The cookie sheet was a jumble of overlapping ovals.

'What are you doing?' I asked.

'Homework,' she replied. She didn't bother to look up at me because it didn't matter. To her I was just a smudge with a voice. 'One of the bad things about being home-schooled is that you are always doing homework. And as you know, Mom is always trying to turn every little moment into a lesson. She's making angel halo sugar cookies for the church fair, but at the same time she has turned this into a maths lesson. Now I have to figure out how many cookies I can get per sheet.' She stamped at the sheet and then pressed a button on her calculator, which was the size of a Monopoly box and had a voice that spoke out the numbers as she pressed them.

'Can I help you?' I asked.

'Why? she replied, sounding a bit testy,

like she always does because she is so touchy. 'Why? Do you think I can't do this just because I can't see your twitchy-jumpy-hyper ferret face?'

I wished Mrs Lapp had never told her about my ADHD.

'It's just that at the rate you are going, you'll have a hundred cookie pieces per sheet.'

'What do you know about maths?' she asked, and stared hard at me with her glassy eyes wide open like twin telescopes pointing into outer space.

'I know a lot,' I said. 'Try me.'

'OK,' she said. 'Here's a test. If Pablo barks at a rate of two and a half barks every three seconds, how many barks will he bark in an hour?'

'Do I have an hour to answer this?' I asked.

'Take your time, Einstein,' she taunted.

I knelt down and pulled Pablo out of my backpack. 'OK,' I whispered in his ear. 'You better have eaten your Wheaties.' I pointed at the kitchen clock. 'Ready,' I said to him, 'go.' Then I began to chase Pablo, and he started barking and running in tight little circles and he sounded like a doggy tap dancer with his nails tapping away on the tile floor and I tried to keep count of how many barks he barked for a minute and then I would multiply that by sixty, but I kept losing my place because I kept lunging at him to keep him going and pulling on his tail and blowing into his face and before long I really didn't care how many barks he barked but it was a lot.

Just then Olivia's mother marched into the kitchen. 'Joey,' she said in a voice most people use when ordering a dog around, 'W.W.J.D.?'

'Use a tape recorder,' I said right back, because I figured it would be easier to count the barks if I didn't have to chase him at the same time.

'Joey,' she said, and made a frown out of her whole face. 'I told you not to bring Pablo to school. You know he is very disruptive.'

'Yes, Mrs Lapp,' I said. 'I'll take him home.' I knew Mrs Lapp didn't allow Pablo in her house, which is why I began to sneak him in so then I could get caught and have to take him home where I could sit around and watch TV soaps with Grandma and make soap opera star labels like BACK STABBER and SCARY FACELIFT and CON MAN and GOLD DIGGER and INSANE TWIN SISTER and LONG-LOST HUSBAND and stick them on the screen. I always wore GREY WHINER on my forehead, and Grandma wore EVIL NANNY on her sweatshirt because if she stuck it to her body it would peel her skin off when she removed it.

Only after Mrs Lapp called looking for me would I have to go back. It was a good trick and would give me a break from Olivia.

But Olivia had caught on. 'I'm going too,' she insisted.

'If I go by myself,' I said to Mrs Lapp, 'it will just take me a minute.'

'It's time for morning recess anyway,' Olivia pointed out. 'I want to go.'

Mrs Lapp seemed relieved and glanced up at the clock. 'Sure, why don't you two guys take Pablo home? But come right back.'

Olivia hopped up and made a beeline for her bedroom. On the way she hit the kitchen doorjamb with her hip, and I saw her wince as she crossed the living room. I knew it had to hurt because a few weeks ago we were in a hot tub in the backyard and she had a bathing suit on and both her hips down to her knees were all bruised up, red and purple. I thought maybe her mom spanked her on one side while her dad spanked her on the other, and when I asked, she laughed. 'No. My parents don't *spank* me. I'm the one with the disability, so I get to spank them.'

'Oh,' I said.

'They aren't like your parents,' she said. 'Both of yours are nuts, and your grand-mother sounds creepy.'

Ever since I told her about me and my family, she wouldn't stop teasing me. That didn't bother me too much because she was so mean about her own family who I thought were really nice to her. Her mother waited on her like a slave, and her dad was some-thing off an old TV show where the people are so nice they aren't real. He was a big-rig truck driver who was only home on week-ends, and when he arrived on Fridays, she made him carry her everywhere as if she were his personal cargo. He was one of those skinny guys with a pot belly like pizza dough, and she locked her arms around his neck and hooked her long stringbean legs behind his knees, and from a distance they looked like Siamese twins staggering around the house.

When she returned from her room she was wearing a bicycle helmet, an orange reflector sash, knee pads, and elbow pads.

'Don't dawdle,' her mom said as we went outside. 'I want to work on fractions when you come back.'

'I'll do my best,' I said, and gave her a crooked smile, because there was just no way to hustle Olivia along.

When we went outside, she walked so slowly down the sidewalk, it was as if her Buster Brown shoes were the noses of two bloodhounds sniffing out an escapee. She walked with one hand sticking straight out like a sleepwalker, and the other held her cane so she could smack me on the leg and make sure I hadn't run off because it was really hard for me to move so slowly.

'Why do you put up with me?' she asked, and hit me on the leg.

'I need a friend,' I said.

She laughed. 'And you expect *me* to be your friend?'

'Yes,' I said.

'Well, if you are going to be my friend, you

have to know what I hate,' she said. 'Knowing what I hate is more important than knowing what I love.'

'I don't want to know what you hate,' I said. 'Really.'

'Then you'll never be my friend,' she said. 'Because most of who I am is defined by what I don't like.'

'I always thought it was harder to choose what you did like than what you didn't,' I said.

'No, you have it backward, as usual,' she said harshly.

'You sound a lot like my grandma,' I said. 'I think you two have a lot in common. You should meet.'

'So do you want to know what I hate?' she asked, and raised her cane up over my head. 'Or are you just going to jabber on?'

I flinched. 'Tell me,' I said.

'I hate that everyone tries to help me. I mean help me with everything. You'd think I was retarded – not blind. I'd rather get hit and flattened by my dad's semi than have one more stranger grab me by the collar and jerk me out of my shoes and back onto the sidewalk every time I step off a kerb.'

'OK,' I said, 'but it is nice that somebody wants to help you.'

'No, it's not,' she said. 'It's like being a little kid for ever. It's like they want to seal me up in one of those clear plastic balls like a scorpion or put me into one of those wintry snow domes and give me a shake every Christmas.'

'I like Christmas,' I said.

She threw back her head and groaned. 'You sound just like my mom. She likes *everything* cute. It's disgusting. Anytime I say I don't like something, she tells me to cheer up and think of life on the bright side. That's usually when I remind her that I'm blind and couldn't *see* the bright side even if I wanted to.'

Listening to her was making every muscle in my body tense up, as if a boa constrictor were trying to crush my ribs. 'I'll be right back,' I gasped. I took off running down the street as fast as I could and my mind was racing a mile a minute and I was thinking that Grandma wanted me to make a friend and here I was in a classroom where there was only *one* other student and she was about the most unfriendly person I had ever

74

met and I had no idea how to win her over because being a secret helper superhero was getting me nowhere. And all I could wish for was to return to my old school and get back into my classroom and meet some nice kids and try to have a life that was all about what people liked instead of what they hated.

When I returned she was standing on her tiptoes with her face high up in the air feeling the breeze blow across her skin. I wanted to ask her if the wind felt like butterfly wings, but then I knew she would snap at me so I kept my mouth shut and just stared at her. But she must have heard me return.

'I can feel you staring at me,' she growled. 'that's another thing I hate. People who *stare*.'

'Sorry,' I said and stared at Pablo instead.

When we got to my house, I asked if she wanted to come in.

'Why?' she snapped. 'I thought you were just going to ditch your dog then skip school.'

'We can't do that,' I said. 'Now just come in and meet my grandmother.'

'Why?'

'Because it would be a special favour to me if you told her we were good friends.'

'But I'm not your friend,' she snarled. 'A real friend would skip school with me.'

'Please tell her we're friends. She's sick and it would really cheer her up.'

'We're all sick,' she said.

'Some of us are sicker than others,' I replied, and had to bite my tongue to keep from calling her the sickest one of all.

'I make it a rule to never cheer anyone up,' she declared.

'Then you should really get to know my grandma. Like I said, you have more in common with her than you do with me.'

She shrugged, then turned around and tapped back down the sidewalk a little ways. 'Aren't you coming?' she asked, without turning towards me.

'I have to go feed Pablo,' I said. 'You be the tortoise and I'll be the hare and we'll see who gets back to your house first.'

She stuck her nose up in the air and tapped away.

As soon as I stepped inside Grandma grabbed me by the arm and spooked me. She'd been watching us through the curtain.

'Why didn't you invite her in?' she rasped.

'I did,' I said with a groan. 'She's not ready.'

'Well, I wish you'd bring me a friend,' she said. 'I'm so tired, I may not have enough energy to die properly and I'll just shrivel up into a zombie. And if I do, I promise you I'll haunt you for the rest of your life.'

I believed her. 'Stop it,' I said. I trotted to the kitchen to give Pablo some food before I left him.

'Do you want some advice on making friends?' Grandma wheezed from the doorway. 'I'm good at making friends.'

'I don't need help,' I said as I hustled past her. She stumbled back against the wall and let out a zombie wail. 'Sorry!' I hollered as I ran outside and down the street. I was afraid Olivia might have run off, but she was still tapping her way along the sidewalk. I sneaked around her and was silently waiting at her front door when she arrived.

'Beat you,' I said when she was a foot away. I stuck out my face and reached for her hand. I wanted to rub it across my toothy grin as if it were a smile in braille.

Instead, she lifted her cane and smacked

me across the shoulder. 'Beat you too,' she said nastily. 'Now get out of my way.'

If only I could.

4.
Mr Helpful

I love Saturdays. They are my best thinking days. It is my day to try to find that one special thought that turns into an idea that I remember for ever and becomes a part of who I am, like a freckle or a finger or an ear. Even before I open my eyes I take a deep breath and try to picture something, anything, as if my brain were a keyhole where I can spy on my future. So each Saturday morning I try to find a little piece of a thought, and then I keep turning it over in my mind until it turns into a complete idea and at the end of the day when I'm lying in bed I put the whole thought into a little room in my head so I can remember it.

When I woke up Grandma was still asleep and Mom wasn't around because she had got up extra early to help Booth serve breakfast down at the homeless shelter. Now that it was getting colder, a lot of homeless people needed more help. I tiptoed out back and got a hammer and a bunch of big nails out of the toolbox, then went back to my bedroom. I closed my door and pounded enough of them into the wall over my bed until I could get Dad's crushed silencer to stay up there. It looked really cool. Then suddenly my morning thought popped into my head as if I had hit myself with the hammer: 'Why do I want the silencer on my wall, since it only reminds me how crazy Dad and Mom are?' Obviously, that question was the little piece of a thought for me to work on. I took my label gun and squeezed out WHAT DOES THIS MEAN? and stuck it to the bottom of the silencer so when I was in bed I could look up and read it.

When I went back into the living room, Grandma was awake too.

'Were you beating your head against the wall?' she asked.

'No,' I said. 'But I was wondering. Do you think I'm weird because I'm wired, or wired because I'm weird?'

'Which came first, the chicken or the egg?' Grandma asked.

'Nobody knows the answer to that,' I said. I began to squeeze out a WEIRD OR WIRED label while Grandma kept talking.

'Same thing with your question,' she replied. 'Nobody knows, though I've been trying to figure it out from where I'm sitting.' She patted the couch. 'Think of it this way,' she said. 'Each day when my curtain opens, it is like watching you all on stage. I get to sit here like I'm in a theatre while you all go in and out of doors, pace the floors, yell and rant and rave and go nuts in front of me all day long. That's how I see all this chasing around back and forth, and believe me, I don't know if you were born nuts to begin with or if you make each other nuts with the way you treat each other. I just don't know, and probably never will. But it couldn't hurt if you all were nicer to each other.'

'I'm nice,' I said, and pressed my WEIRD OR WIRED label onto my forehead. 'I want to help everyone be nice. That's all I want to do. Just help. That's my whole thing now. I'm Mr Helpful.' I began to squeeze out a MR HELPFUL label.

'I think you are Mr Out-of-Your-Mind,' she said. 'Stop trying to help everyone.'

'I'm trying to help you,' I said. 'I'm trying to turn Olivia into a friend although she really upsets me because she's so mean.'

'You know, Joey, if you didn't wear those med patches, you'd just be thinking about yourself, and you wouldn't care about making everyone happy. Your problem is that you got better, and the rest of the world didn't.'

'And that's why I'm trying to help the whole world,' I said. 'Because now I can.'

'No, you can't,' she said. 'You can't do anything for a person who is stuck between being happy and being miserable. All you can do is get trapped in the middle, and anyone in the middle just gets squished.'

'Then what should I do?' I asked.

'Go up to the discount grocery store and get me some scratch tickets,' she said, and held out a few dollars.

'Mom says that's a waste of money,' I replied. 'You should save it.'

'Save it for what?' she shot back, and began to hack away into a huge handkerchief that was wadded up like a turban. 'Right now my life is a lottery. I'm so old, the state won't give me new lungs. The only way I am going to get a transplant is to buy them outright. So winning the lottery is the last chance I have of staying alive.'

'I hate it when you talk about dying,' I said.

'Well, you better get used to it,' she replied. 'Because I'm going down the tubes, and fast. I got more fluid than air in my lungs. You want to listen? Put your ear against me, and I swear you can hear the ocean better in my chest than you can in a seashell.'

She started to pull up her shirt, and I looked the other way.

'OK, OK,' I begged with my hands over my eyes. 'Pull down your shirt. I'll get the tickets.'

She reached forward and shoved the money into my back pocket and I scooped Pablo off the stuffed chair.

'One more thing,' she said, and waved me over to her side.

'What?'

She reached forward and ripped the WEIRD OR WIRED label off my forehead.

'Ow!' I shrieked. 'You pulled out some of my brain with that!'

'Believe me,' she said, tossing the label over her shoulder, 'you don't need to advertise what is already so obvious about your brain. Now *git*!'

I bolted for the door and down the steps, and up Plum Street. I ran over to the old ice factory, where during the summer I hugged the walls and stuck a COOL SPOT TO HUG label on a metal door because it *was* the coldest spot in town. Then I ran under the railroad bridge and touched my BEWARE! SCARY OLD GOAT MAN label, because at night some man sleeps under the bridge and when I pass through on the nights I sneak out my window and walk around town in the dark he's always asking for money.

Another thing I've been trying to do on my walks is to know what I'm looking at, when I'm looking at it. I want to be smart. When I walk down the sidewalk I see about a hundred different kinds of bugs and all I do is point at them like a caveman and say,

'Ugh, look, a bug,' but I know each one of them must have a different name and a different reason why and how it came to be on the planet, and I don't know any of that stuff. I can't even put a proper label on them. I just know one word, *bug*, and it makes me feel like a moron, like I should just have KID stuck to my head. It's like when I hear some people talk and their favourite words are *thing* and *it* – as if they don't know anything by its real name. I wish everything in the world came with a label on it, like all the food I see when I walk down the aisle in the grocery store. Everything there tells me on the outside exactly what is on the inside. Like when I get to the soup section and look at the shelf, each can is not just labelled 'soup', and then I have to shake it and guess at what is inside it. No. Each can says exactly what it is: TOMATO, CHICKEN NOODLE, SPLIT PEA . . . I like that and whenever I'm a little confused about something, I can walk into a grocery store, and because it is so well ordered, my brain gets well ordered. And the best part of all this is, when I know all about everything I am looking at or thinking about, I can imagine how everything works from the beginning all the way to the end. I can think things through, as everybody is always trying to get me to do. Now I can imagine a seed being planted and watered, then sprouting, then growing and turning into a sapling, then a tree that gets bigger and bigger until it flowers and grows more seeds and those seeds fall to the ground, and then they too turn into little trees and before long there is a field of trees, then a country of trees, and then a whole world full of trees. It's like one thought leading to another and another and another, and before long it all adds up to a complete picture of what is going to happen when enough seeds are planted.

When I came out from under the railroad tracks, I crossed the street and went up to the big blue Goodwill donation bin. I liked to hide in it once in a while but today I wanted to check the Goodwill donations before I went to the grocery store because the last time I was at the store there was a lady walking around in just her socks and she looked like she could use some shoes. I went up to her and asked her what size she wore, but she just grunted at me, so now I had to guess and keep a pair on me in case I saw her again.

But when I pushed open the swinging flap on the bin and stuck my head in to check on my JOEY WAS HERE label and look for shoes there was some homeless guy sitting in there and he grabbed my arm and I screamed blue murder and he let go and I backed right out. 'Run!' I yelled to Pablo, and we dashed across the parking lot as fast as we could until we reached the grocery store. Then I remembered that Mom and Booth were helping at the homeless shelter, so I ran back to the Goodwill bin and pushed open the flap with a bent toy baseball bat and yelled. 'You should go down to the shelter and get some food. Ask for Fran!' Then I turned and ran away feeling a lot better because I had helped him out.

The manager of the All-American Discount Grocery Store loves that I come to help out. It's like I work there, but I don't, because I work for free. What I do is first take an empty shopping cart and go up and down each aisle and find all the food that is out of place, and once I have a cart full of food, I get busy returning each item. And while I do this totally relaxing job I can think about all the mixed-up stuff in my own life, because thinking is like taking an out-of-place thought in my brain and putting it in its proper place. If every item in the world and every thought in my brain were in its proper spot, it would be the same as everything in my life being just right. Grandma would get new lungs, Mom and Dad would stop fighting. Olivia would start being my friend, and Pablo would follow my orders like he is supposed to but doesn't always. And I would end up sitting in the front row of Mrs Lucchina's class again, where she could look at me all day and think to herself, 'I wish all my students were as nice and thoughtful and smart and well behaved as that handsome Joey Pigza.'

Before I went into the store, I tucked Pablo under my shirt. It tickled because he was breathing so hard I could feel his breath like little puffs of dragon steam against my belly. I pulled down the neck of my T-shirt and peeked in on him. 'Stop that,' I whispered. 'I have to go check in with the manager.'

Then I marched right up to the manager's cubicle and knocked on his little door, which he never closed.

He didn't look up from the piles of paper on his desk. 'I'm busy!' he shouted.

'It's me, Joey!' I shouted right back. 'Mr Helpful is here to help.'

He turned towards me and smiled. 'Sorry,' he said. 'I'm always happy to see you. But you have to leave the dog outside.' He pointed to my belly.

'How'd you know?' I asked.

'All my training in spotting shoplifters,' he said, and pointed up at the black-and-white security monitors over his desk. 'A lot of people shove stuff under their shirts, especially around the holidays. After a while it's easy to tell what is real belly and what is not.'

'I'll be right back,' I said. I ran out the front door and around to the back of the building, where the big trash dumpsters were parked. I lifted up my shirt and put Pablo on the ground. He started sniffing the grease spots, and I knew if I could find something for him to eat, he'd take a nap and stay put. I dug through some trash boxes and found a lot of rotten vegetables he wouldn't even drool on. Then I spotted a box of old honeydew melons. Pablo loves melon. I picked one up, reared back, and threw it against the wall. It split open and fell to the ground. As soon as he smelled it, he ran over and began to lick the insides. 'Don't eat the seeds,' I warned him, 'or a melon vine will grow inside you.' I turned and looked across the beat-up parking lot. Only a lady in a purple wig and big black boots was picking her way around the holes in the asphalt. She looked harmless. 'See you in a little bit,' I said to Pablo, and headed back to the store.

I grabbed a cart and got started. Because Thanksgiving was only a few days away, the entire store was decorated for the holiday with cardboard turkeys and pumpkins, and plastic corn-on-the-cob, and fake fall leaves.

I started up the first aisle, and when I passed a cardboard cutout of a pilgrim family in those funny top hats and square shoes I started thinking about Mom and Dad and Booth and Grandma, especially Grandma. She had told me she 'saw something ugly heading our way', but wouldn't share it with me. It had to do with what she called the 'law of seven'. She said that when it comes to disasters, there are six awful events and then the seventh is a total catastrophe. I figured if the motorcycle wreck was one, the drinking glass smashing the window was two. And now, as I put an open package of cookies into my basket, I was wondering what number three would be.

As I worried, I strolled up the special-sale section where all the leftover Hallowe'en candy was stacked along with all the spooky plastic pumpkins and fake bloody hands and eyeballs on springs and fang-toothed Draculas and ghosts and glowing skeletons and black Grim Reapers and all the stuff that is really spooky at night but isn't spooky during the day when it is lined up on the shelves with big red mark-down tags all over it. A lot of the world is like this, I thought. It's spooky when you first see it at night when you are out trick-or-treating, but the next day it looks pretty harmless. It was like Grandma. When I was really young and she took care of me, I thought she was the scariest witch on the planet. But now that I'd got to know her she was just some grouchy old ladybug.

Suddenly I heard something that put the fear in me, just as the clock in the crocodile had put the fear in Captain Hook. It was Olivia tapping her way down the aisle. I gasped and did an about-face and ran right into Mrs Lapp.

'Why, Joey,' she said, 'what are you doing here?'

'Bargain hunting,' I whispered as I tried to edge around her.

'Is that Joey?' Olivia shouted. 'What's he doing here?'

'Extra credit,' I said.

'Well, you can give me some extra help,' said Mrs Lapp. 'I forgot my coupons at home. If you and Olivia could stay here while I run and get them, it would be a lot faster for me. OK?'

I was trapped. 'OK,' I said, 'but I'm working my Saturday job.'

'Well, I'm sure Olivia would be happy to help you. Wouldn't you, Olivia?'

She whacked her stick on the floor as if she were scaring away a snake. 'I love to help,' she said.

After Mrs Lapp left I stared at Olivia. If she were an out-of-place product, I'd put her in the frozen food aisle.

'What's your job?' she asked.

'Putting things in their proper place,' I said. 'I tidy up the store.'

'How much do they pay?' she asked.

'I do it for free,' I said. 'It's kind of a hobby. I used to play baseball, but this is better for me.'

'Well, let me help you,' she said sweetly.

'That's nice of you,' I said, but I was suspicious. 'We can work together.'

'That's just what I was thinking,' she replied. Then in a flash she started grabbing things off the shelves and tapping down the aisle and putting the first things she grabbed back in the wrong place and then she grabbed some more stuff and started shoving wrong things everywhere. I had to run behind her and grab the out-of-place stuff, then turn and put it back in its right place, then hurry and catch up to her but by then she had already moved more stuff all around and I was falling behind. And before long I was so far behind I was just running up and down the aisles with my eyes darting across the shelves because I was finding her disasters everywhere. I found a frozen turkey in the potato bin and apples with the dish soap and cans of beans with the toilet paper and no matter how hard I tried to straighten up the confusion, she was ten steps ahead of me and in no time the store was in worse shape than after a week of regular people making a mess.

She made me so nervous, I didn't know what to do. I ran over to the manager's little cubicle. He was busy with a phone call. I stared up at the black-and-white security TVs, and there she was in aisle three, just snatching things left and right and running around and mis-shelving them all over. But then I saw something else. She was *smiling*. And not just her little smirk-smile, but a big huge grin was spread out over her face, and she was laughing so hard even her eyes seemed alive, and I just stood there thinking, Yes, she does laugh. She can have fun. She knows how to have a good time. The store radio was playing the Beatles' 'Yellow Submarine', and her lips were moving as if she was singing it out loud, and she was bopping her head to the beat and tapping her cane as if she were on stage. At that moment I was thankful to be me, because I was the only secret helper spy on the planet who could see behind her mean-girl Hallowe'en mask.

On the monitor I watched her moving to the condiment section, and I took off running for her. As soon as I got close enough, I said, 'I saw you singing on the TV they use for shoplifters. You were smiling too. What's making you so happy?'

She turned towards me and in a real smarmy voice said, 'I'm smiling and singing a happy song because I'm thinking that I'm really screwing up your job and you are probably going to get fired and that would make me the happiest blind girl in the world.'

I was just about to scream *I've had it with you!* when Mrs Lapp appeared and said, 'Oh, there you two are. Was Olivia a big help to you, Joey?'

'Huh?' I said.

'*Huh* is an ugly sound,' she said. 'Now what have you been doing all this time?'

Before I could make up an excuse, Olivia cut in. 'He's been totally hyper, and all he did was run around the store and mix up all the groceries and get into trouble with the manager.'

'That's not true!' I hollered. 'You'll see.' And I marched to the manager's office because I wanted him to tell Mrs Lapp that I wasn't a pain but he wasn't in his office and I looked up at one of the TVs and there I was standing by his door, hopping from foot to foot while wringing my hands with my eyes all bugged out and I *did* look totally hyper and all I could think of was this girl was driving me around the bend just as much as my grandma had and my mom and dad and I had no patience for waiting any longer because it was time to get Pablo and give him a big hug and have him lick my face all over with his stinky rotten melon breath while I settled down. He was the best friend in the world and even if *he* were blind and deaf and had three legs and no teeth and a bent tail he would still love me more than anyone on this planet. And I took off like a rocket out the front door and around back and I was yelling out Pablo's name even before I reached the corner. And then when I turned the corner I was really yelling his name because he was nowhere in sight. 'Pablo!' I hollered with my hands cupped around my mouth. 'Pablo!'

He was gone. I mean he wasn't anywhere. And believe me, I looked in the bushes, in all the dumpsters, in the parking lot. Out in the road. Everywhere. And I couldn't find him, and I knew deep down inside he needed my help and I didn't know what to do, and I was scared because I thought this was definitely disaster number three.

But then I knew exactly what to do, and I went running towards the Beauty and the Beast hair salon because that's where Mom was, and it was her job in life to help me when I couldn't help myself.

'Pablo!' I shouted. 'Pablo!' I ran down the middle of the street shouting his name until some kid jumped out onto his porch and shouted back, 'I'm Pablo. What do you want?'

'Sorry,' I yelled without slowing down. 'Sorry. I'm calling my dog.' And I was sorry. Sorry all over. Soooooo sorry.

'Pablo! Hang on. I'm coming as fast as I can.'

5.

Lost Dog

Mom was slumped down with her eyes closed in a special seat with one of those aluminium dome hairdryers covering the top of her head.

'Mom!' I shouted above the humming. But I knew from playing with the machines that she couldn't hear me.

I picked up a hairbrush and banged on the side of it. 'Mom!' I shouted again. *Bang. Bang. Bang.*

She lifted the dome and I almost cracked her on the ear. 'What?' she asked, and snatched the brush away. 'What are you doing here?'

'Pablo's been stolen!' I said and tugged on her smock, which was smeared with different colours of smelly hair dye.

'Joey, nobody would steal that dog.'

'But, Mom—'

'Joey, don't start with the dramatics. I've had a bad enough day. You know what happened?'

'I don't want to know,' I said. 'Not now. Pablo is missing, and the longer he is gone, the harder it will be to find him. Come on.'

'No,' she said. 'I'm not going anywhere. I'm going to sit here and fry my brain under this dome until my headache goes away. You know what your dad did today?'

'I don't have time,' I said. 'Pablo's been stolen. Or he's way lost. We have to act fast.'

'Your dad dressed up in women's clothes and marched in here with his hips swinging back and forth like a tart, and he was wearing some god-awful frilly lavender wig—'

'Stop,' I said. 'Listen to me!'

'— so he goes up to Tiffany and says, "I'm lookin' to make an appointment with Fran to do something with this mop on my head." So Tiffany comes and gets me and says a clown is here who needs some big-time help, so I think, well, maybe the circus is in town, but when I go out there and take a good look, I could see right away it was your father dressed like a beat-up Barbie.'

'Mom, I don't want to hear this,' I said.

'Well, who else can I tell this stuff to? He's your father. You should know what kind of nut he is.'

'I already know,' I said. 'He's a *nut*. He'll always be a nut.'

'Well, he's driving me nuts too.'

'Mom,' I begged, tugging at her apron. 'this isn't about you goin' nuts. This is about me goin' nuts because Pablo is missing.'

'And then your dad rips off his weirdo wig and drops down on one knee and takes out some see-through plastic shoe that he must have bought in a costume shop and grabs my foot. He scared me half to death. Then he yanks my shoe off and jams the plastic shoe on me and says, "You are my Cinderella. Come with me to my castle where we'll live happily ever after" – or some such nonsense. I thought I'd never breathe again, I was so stunned. So he bends down to kiss my foot, and I just kicked him as hard as I could, and he grabs his chin and yells out that I've hurt him again and that – get this – I'm the evil one! I thought I'd take my scissors and cut his heart out and feed it to the danged rats.'

'M-a-a-a!' I moaned, and poked myself in the chest. 'Listen to me. Me! Me! Me! Pablo has been stolen. We have to call the police and start finding him right away.'

'Oh, I'm sure Pablo'll come back,' she said, and snapped her fingers. 'He'll get hungry and come home. Just set out some food for him. There's no reason to get overexcited.'

She looked away for a moment, and her eyes were as empty as Olivia's. Then she stooped down, and I caught her glancing at her watch before she began to speak. 'I'm so glad you came in today. I was going to go looking for you, because I have something important to tell you. After your dad's little stunt, I've decided I should stay at Booth's place for a short while,' she said. 'I need to chill, and anyway Booth and I need some time to figure out what we're doing with each other, and all the commotion that's going on around the house is too much for us right now.'

'Wait a minute. What about me?' I asked.

'You know, me. You love me more than him. Think of me. I already lost Pablo and now I'm losing you.'

'You aren't losing me, honey, I'm still here. But I'm trying to move on with my life too. Can't you understand that?'

'No, I can't,' I said. 'Why do you have to move on without me?'

She paused, and then she said something that was like magic words sprinkled over my head.

'Help me,' she said. 'I need you to help me by being strong for yourself right now. I need you to buck up and do all the right things.'

'But I need *you*,' I said. 'I'm just a boy.'

'You are my *big* boy,' she said, 'so you shouldn't sound like such a baby. Grandma is here now. You and she get along great. In fact, you said yourself that you two think alike. So you'll be fine. I already told her this morning, and she said she looks forward to being with you. It'll be like old times, she said.'

Which old times? I thought. The ones where Grandma made me behave like a dog and do doggy tricks? Or the ones where I was her baby and she protected me from

Mom and Dad as they jumped in and out of our lives like escaped mental patients?

'And what about Dad?' I blurted out. 'He's zipping around all over the place.'

'That's another thing I wanted to tell you. I called the cops and Booth is going to take me down to the station so I can get a restraining order against him. Honey, he's after me. Not you. So don't worry. Once I'm out of the house, he'll go away too.'

I just stood there feeling like a big exclamation mark swelling up and up and up and was about to burst until I shouted, 'I can't believe you really think leaving me behind is a good idea!'

'It's just for a little while,' she said. 'Once I figure out what I want, we'll all be better off. Someday you'll understand that.'

'I understand that *now*!' I shouted. 'That's easy to understand. What I don't understand is why you are more interested in Booth than you are in me because I can help you more than he ever can. I'd help you do *anything*.'

Her eyes broke away from mine, and she looked over my head.

'Hi, Fran,' Booth said. 'Heck of a day, isn't it? Hi, Joey.'

I turned and frowned at him. 'Go away,' I said. 'Leave us alone.'

'Is this a bad time?' he asked Mom.

'It's always a bad time to steal my mother,' I said. 'She's mine.' I reached out for her, but she reached me first and held my shoulder. In a moment she had steered me into the storeroom at the salon.

'Joey,' she said with her long nails pressing into my shoulder, 'we can do this the easy way or the hard way. You know I love you. Give me a little space to work this out with Booth, and then we'll all get back on track.'

'No,' I said loudly. I jerked my shoulder away from her hand because it was my shoulder, just like my heart was mine and I didn't want it in her hands either. I lowered my head, knowing she was going to do what she wanted no matter what I did. Then I thought of one last thing. 'He can come stay with us,' I said in a whisper. 'You can work it all out at our house. I'll be good. I'll be very, very good. I'll listen to Booth and do everything he asks. I won't argue. I won't do anything weird. I'll be the perfect helper.'

'You're perfect already,' she said, reaching out to touch my face.

'If I'm so perfect, why are you doing this?'

Booth opened the door and stuck his head in. 'Fran,' he said, 'we have to get going. They're waiting for us at the station.'

'OK,' she replied. 'We'll just be a minute more.' She raised one finger in the air.

I looked at the finger and thought, That's what I am now – one minute of her time.

'Booth and I have to get going, hon. We can finish talking about this later.'

'Later, when?' I asked, and stomped my foot down.

Booth stuck his head back in. 'Joey,' he said in that fake dad's voice he gets when his patience runs out, 'do as your mother tells you to do.'

At that moment I wanted to slam the door shut across his neck.

'You are stealing my mother,' I said as under control as I possibly could. 'Someone just stole my dog, and now you are stealing my mother. I should call the cops on *you*.'

He didn't even say anything. He reached for my mom's hand, and she reached for his and stood up.

'Joey,' she said, 'just settle down in here for a minute, and when you've calmed down, I want you to go straight home, and I'll call you tonight.'

'Can't I go look for Pablo?' I asked.

'Go home and put some food out for him,' she suggested. 'That will do the trick. Besides, your dad is out there running around like a nut so I'd feel better if you were at home.'

'OK,' I said, and lowered my head. 'I'll do what you want even if you like someone else more.'

'Don't worry,' she whispered. 'I'll always love you the most.' Then she closed the door. But, when it clicked shut, I felt something in me click shut too. It was my heart, and it was locking her out, and it was locking me in, and that was about the worst feeling I ever had. I sat down on the floor and leaned forward so my knees covered my ears. I didn't want to hear anything. I held my nose so I couldn't smell anything. I closed my eyes so I couldn't see anything. I didn't want to touch anything or taste anything. I was trying to imagine how to be *nothing* – not dead, just relieved, like a sharp pain that finally disappeared.

Then after a minute of being quiet, I whispered to myself, 'What would Joey do?' – not the old wired Joey, but the new helpful Joey. The big-boy Joey. The better-than-a-boyfriend Joey.

'Unlock your heart,' I answered. 'She needs you. She said so herself. So don't flip out. Be strong.'

And as soon as my heart unlocked and I took a deep breath as if I had been let out of a dungeon, I remembered it was Pablo who needed my help right now. Mom had Booth. Pablo was all alone. 'Pablo!' I shouted. 'Hang on, I'm coming!' And I hopped up and burst out of the storeroom and ran up the street looking down at the asphalt as I went because the first thing I thought was that he might be roadkill. I ran up and down nearly all of Lancaster before going home, and my heart nearly burst half a dozen times because I thought I found him flattened out, but it was only dead squirrels, which are about the same size.

When I got home, I ran over to the telephone. I thought I'd call everyone in town and tell them to be on the lookout for Pablo.

I flipped the phone book to the yellow pages and started with the AAAA Driving School. When they answered, I told them about Pablo and asked if they wouldn't mind keeping student drivers off the road until I found him. They hung up on me.

I called A-OK Septic Service. They hung up. I called A-1 Locksmith. Then Angie's Touch-of-Class Nails and Tanning. Some kid laughed through his nose and hung up. I was calling Arthur's Beverage Sales when Grandma yanked the phone out of my hand.

'Enough,' she croaked. 'Do yourself a favour and put on a fresh patch. No, make it a double. You're acting like your old self again. And I don't like that. But what makes me really mad is that the nuts in this family are bringing out the worst in you again. They should be ashamed, but they're not because they are too selfish to think of anyone's needs other than their own.'

I lowered my head. 'Help me, Grandma,' I said. 'What should I do?'

'Go take care of your meds, and then we'll make some LOST DOG signs and you can tack them up around the neighbourhood. That'll help. And we'll call the dog pound too.'

When I returned from my bedroom, Grandma was just hanging up the phone. 'I talked to a lady at the pound,' she said. 'Three other people are missing Chihuahuas. Now what do you think the odds are for a town this small to suddenly lose four Chihuahuas in one day?'

'A million to one?' I guessed. 'Two million to one? Three million?'

'Hey, that reminds me,' Grandma said. 'Where are my scratch tickets? Maybe I'll win a million, and we can buy a hundred and one Chihuahuas.'

'I forgot them,' I said. 'I'm sorry.'

'Well, run back out there and get 'em,' she said. 'It'll do you good to work off some of that wired energy you got pent up.'

I shot out of the house. Grandma may have been right about Pablo. He's only a dog. But not just any dog. He's a mutt with mostly Chihuahua blood, which meant he's small enough to be one of my body parts like a heart or liver with little ears and a tail. It's like he was part of me just like east is connected to west. He doesn't wake up wanting a new human, and I don't wake up wanting a new dog. He has been with me ever since I got out of special ed. and he is my lucky charm, and when I rub his belly, good things do happen, and I wished his belly was with me now. And while I stood in line at the grocery store to get the tickets the lady in front of me had a milk carton with a missing kid on it. Everybody cared about a missing kid. But nobody cared if there was one less Chihuahua in the world. No one. And I wondered if Pablo was feeling and thinking the same thing, and that made me even sadder because I know when you feel that no one cares about you, then before long it is easy to care less and less about yourself until you are a speck without a voice.

After I got the tickets, I walked out back and checked by the dumpsters one more time just in case he had got lost, or was trapped under a box of toppled garbage, or had eaten too much and had fallen asleep like everyone does after Thanksgiving, or had chased after some big dogs and had returned to the dumpsters and was waiting patiently to tell me all about it – when I heard Dad's motorcycle coming. I turned towards him and watched as he sped past the Goodwill bin and across the grocery store parking lot and headed right for me. He had his dark glasses on and looked as blind and mean as Olivia, and I thought he might run me down, but at the last moment he turned away.

'Dad!' I shouted, and waved my arms as he roared past with his cut-up leathers flapping in the breeze. 'Dad, stop! I need your help!' But he went right on by and through the old stockyard gates behind the store and disappeared into the dark maze of pens that Grandma told me had been around from when she was a kid – only then the pens were full of cattle that were shipped in and out on the train.

On my way home I walked across the broken sidewalks, past all the shifty gnomes, and I was thinking about Pablo and what he would say if he was a human. As a dog he mostly barks at everything. I imagine that if he was a person, he would be a lot like Grandma, always telling people what to do and how to live and where to go, and he would just be yapping off a long list of nonstop opinions about how dogs and people should behave properly and how the world should be run to suit him. And I figured whoever stole him would soon want to get rid of him because it took an especially patient person like me to really put up with an especially difficult dog like Pablo.

6.

WANTED MAN

When my eyelids flipped open the next morning, I looked up at the silencer on the wall above my head, and it seemed to me that I put it on the wall because that was exactly how I felt – burned out and flattened and miserable. Maybe that was what it meant. But I didn't have time to think about it because Pablo was still missing. I crawled under my covers and down to the end of my mattress where he had dug out a little cave for himself, but he wasn't in it. He was gone.

I got up and went into the living room. Grandma's curtain was already open, and she was smoking a cigarette and flipping through the phone book.

'Pablo missing is bad thing number three,' I said.

'Well, hold onto your seat,' she advised. 'You got four to go before blast-off.'

'What should I do?' I asked.

'Go get your friend and start looking for him. Tomorrow I'll call around to all the vets and dog dealers and pet stores and places where he might have ended up,' she announced. 'They won't be open today since it's Sunday.'

'But Olivia's driving me crazy,' I whined.

'The best of friends always start off by driving each other nuts,' she said.

'But I already have Dad and Mom and Pablo and you,' I replied. 'Don't you think I already have enough friends who drive me nuts?'

'Your dad is insane, your mom is distracted, Pablo has a brain the size of a grain of sand, and I'll soon be out of your hair, so it's good that someone else is testing you out.'

'But I'm enough of a test all by myself,' I wailed.

Just then there was a knock on the door. Not many people ever knocked on our door, and when they did, it was usually bad news. But I was sure this would be good news. I was sure that someone had found Pablo. I leaped at the door and yanked it open.

It was a cop.

'Is he dead?' I blurted out. 'Is he?'

'Who?' the cop asked. 'Who's dead?'

'My dog, Pablo.'

'I don't know anything about a dog,' he replied. 'I'm here to take a boy named' – he looked down at a piece of paper – 'Joey Pigza down to the station.'

I looked over at Grandma with so much fear, I could feel myself turning to stone. She winked at me. 'I'll go get Joey,' Grandma said to the cop, pulling her pyjama top over her head. 'You just wait on the porch.'

'OK,' he said. And when he stepped back, I gently closed the door.

'What do I do?' I whispered.

'As I told you before, Joey,' she said, 'you better take care of yourself because nobody can tell what your parents are up to. Now they set the cops on you.'

'Should I crawl under the couch?' I asked.

'No. Go to the Lapps',' she said. 'Scram. I'll get rid of the cop.'

I grabbed my backpack and ran out the back door and across our yard and into the cemetery, and all along I felt as if my bottom were being poked with a long pin. I cut in front of the statue of Jesus and out the other side and down and around the block until I saw a bunch of people waiting for a bus, and I just hung around them for a few minutes having a fake conversation with myself like I was someone's kid until I caught my breath, which I didn't because even standing still was exhausting me, and then I headed for Olivia's house.

Along the way I picked up a newspaper off of a yard because the Lapps didn't get one and I wanted to look through the Lost and Found columns. I pulled out the Around Town and Classified sections and shoved them into my backpack and left the rest of the paper behind.

When I rang the Lapps' doorbell, I knew exactly what I wanted to say to Mrs Lapp.

'Good morning, Joey,' she sang. 'How nice to see you. We're going to have family Bible study as soon as Mr Lapp gets back from his church duties, and you are welcome to join us. Now, what would Jesus do?'

'Hide under the bed,' I said.

'Now, Joey,' she asked. 'Why would Jesus hide?'

'The police were after him?'

'You mean the Romans,' she said, correcting me. 'Perhaps this is the Bible lesson we should go over.'

'Yes,' I said, 'because I'd like to know how he escaped.'

'*He* went to heaven,' Mrs Lapp said matter-of-factly. 'And *they* were not invited.'

As soon as I entered the house, I went directly into the bathroom and locked the door. I pulled out the newspaper. There were no Chihuahuas in the Dogs Found column. But under Dogs Missing there were three Chihuahuas, just as Grandma had said. One was named Baxter, last seen in his corner yard at Walnut and Lime. The second was named Rita and was last seen tied up to a mailbox outside Zimmerman's Café. The third was named Charro and was last seen chasing a red rubber ball down the street and around the corner by the Turkey Hill Mini Mart.

I folded up the paper and ran out to Olivia. Even though I knew she was going to be mean to me, I *had* to talk to someone or I'd explode. She was sitting at the kitchen table listening to her tape player. I plucked the earphones off her head.

'I'm a wanted man,' I whispered. 'The cops are after me.'

'Is there a reward?' she asked, smiling.

'I don't know,' I said. I explained everything to her about my mom hiding out at Booth's place and Pablo being stolen and how the other dogs were stolen too. 'Maybe the cops think I stole the dogs.'

'Maybe they think you are a serial Chihuahua snatcher,' she suggested. 'Maybe they think you have a bizarre medical lab in your basement and are doing experiments on what makes things small, and yappy, and nervous.'

'Hey,' I said. 'Pablo isn't yappy.'

'I was thinking of you, nitwit,' she replied. 'Now, what else is in the paper?'

I looked at the Around Town section. There was no article about a dog-napper on the loose but I found something else. A bunch of Amish teenage boys and girls had been arrested for drinking. It seemed they had all got together and secretly rented an apartment where they kept regular clothes and had a car and played loud music and drank beer, then sneaked back to their farms and put on their bib overalls and dresses and played like everything was Amish as usual. But the night before, they had played their music too loud, and when the police arrived, they arrested the whole bunch and took them home to their farms. Now they were in big trouble with their parents.

'What do you think of that?' I asked Olivia after reading it to her.

'Looks to me like everyone wants a secret life,' she remarked.

'I don't,' I said. 'With me, what you see is what you get.'

'Well, I want one,' she said. 'Anyone who is not allowed to make mistakes has to live a secret life.'

'I don't have that problem,' I said. 'People expect me to make mistakes.'

'Well, walk a mile in my shoes,' she said.

Suddenly Mrs Lapp was behind me. 'Joey,' she said sharply, and removed the paper from my hands. 'I thought I made it clear we don't read newspapers in this house. Now, why don't you two get some snacks while I brush up on today's lesson on the Roman persecution of Jesus.'

As soon as Mrs Lapp left the room, I started getting jumpy. I couldn't take not knowing what was happening to Pablo. 'I gotta get out of here,' I said to Olivia. 'I have to find Pablo.'

'I'll help if you take me with you,' she said.

'OK,' I agreed. 'But if I go outside, I'll need a disguise. The cops might spot me.'

'I have an extra cane and sunglasses,' she said. 'You can use them and play blind.'

'But how do we got out of here?'

'I'll set off a bomb,' she said. 'Watch.'

I didn't know what she meant. She walked over to the refrigerator and opened the door. She pulled out a big jar of pickles with both hands, turned her face away, and let it drop. It smashed, with glass and pickles and juice flying everywhere. Mrs Lapp was there in seconds.

'What's wrong?' she asked breathlessly, and then saw the floor. 'Are you two OK?'

Olivia started crying, which she was very

good at faking. 'Joey wanted a pickle snack, and the jar slipped out of my hands,' she blubbered. 'It just slipped.'

'That's OK, honey,' her mom said. 'Did you get hit?'

'Only in my eyes,' Olivia said. 'I've been blinded.'

Mrs Lapp looked heavenward and took a deep breath. 'You two go take a stroll while I clean this up,' she said.

As soon as Olivia got all dressed in her special protective outfit and we went outside, I said to her, 'That wasn't nice.'

'What?' she replied.

'Hurting your mother's feelings,' I said. 'Saying you had been blinded.'

'Oh, give me a break,' she said. 'At least my mother loves me enough to put up with me. Yours has run off with someone else.'

'She's just hiding from my dad,' I said. 'She'll be home soon.'

I didn't say anything more after that because my mind began to drift, and for a moment I could imagine coming home to a note from Mom telling me she had run off with Booth. She had run away from me before, and everyone knows doing something a second time is even easier than the first.

Once we were down the street, Olivia unfolded a second red-and-white cane and gave it to me. Then she pulled out a pair of dark glasses. I put them on.

'How do I look?' I asked.

'Don't be a jerk,' she said. 'Now what's our plan?'

'First, we have to go to make sure the cops have left my house. Then we'll get the signs my grandma made and put them up all over town. And while we're putting up the signs, we can keep our eyes open for suspicious dog-nappers.'

'Funny,' she said sarcastically. 'I'll keep my ears open.'

When we got to my house the cop car was gone. 'Let's go,' I said.

She sat down on the front steps. 'You can't trick me into meeting your grandma,' she said. 'I'll wait outside.'

'Look,' I replied. 'My grandmother is sick. Just tell her you are my friend. You don't have to be my friend, but if you were, it would do you some good.'

'It would be a lie if I told her we were friends.'

'Then lie,' I said.

'W.W.J.D.?' she sang in a snotty way.

'He wouldn't have to lie,' I said. 'He'd be my friend. I'm a kid. He likes kids. It's the adults that drove him to his grave.'

'I refuse to lie,' she said.

I ran up the steps pulling at my hair. I just wanted to run in and run out, but Grandma grabbed me as soon as I opened the door.

'What's she doing on the steps?' she asked.

'She won't come in,' I said. 'Believe me, I tried.'

'What have you done to annoy her?'

'Nothing,' I said. 'Honest.'

'Well, you better hurry up and reel her in,' she said. 'I'm already turning into a zombie. I scared that cop away when I told him I was your *mummy*.'

She laughed, then coughed at her own joke, but I wasn't feeling very funny.

'What did he want?' I asked.

'You,' she replied. 'Said he had orders to pick you up.'

'For what?'

'For not helping your grandma and making that girl your friend.'

I spun away from her and ran into my bedroom and got my label marker and all the dog sign stuff I needed except for the tacks. I didn't have any but figured there'd be a lot of them in the telephone poles, and I could recycle them.

Grandma was standing in front of the door wheezing like a fish out of water.

'I'm still *trying*,' I said to her. 'She can't resist me much longer. I promise.'

The moment I stepped out the door, I felt like a whole different person, as if I were one person playing two parts in a really strange movie.

'OK,' I said to Olivia. 'Let's put up a sign on every telephone pole in Lancaster.'

'Whatever you say,' she said. 'I'm blind following the blind.'

'I've been waiting for you to say that,' I said.

We started tap, tap, tapping our way down the street. Then we'd stop at a telephone pole, and since I'd chewed my fingernails down to nothing, I'd pull a used tack out with my teeth like a beaver and tap, tap, tap a sign up. Then I'd squat down and stick a PABLO COME HOME label at dog height on the pole just in case Pablo knew how to read but had been keeping it to himself.

After a while we worked our way over to the street with my old school.

'That's where I went to school before Mom sent me to your house.'

'Did you like going there?'

'Yes,' I said. 'I miss it.'

'Well, I have the perfect plan for how you can get back.'

'What's that?' I asked.

'It's your turn to be mean to me,' she said. 'You can be the bad kid, and I can be the good kid. You can lead me astray and be a bad influence, and when Mom finds out how awful you are, she'll ban you from our house, and you can go back to regular school.'

'I'm not going to cause trouble on purpose,' I said. 'I only do good things to help.'

'Think of it this way,' she said. 'You don't have to be bad to me. You can just be bad around the house until my mom kicks you out. I think you should just be a pain in the neck – you know, be hyper and run around and trash the house and knock me down the stairs a few times so that Mom changes her mind about you and then you can go back to your old school.'

I took a deep breath. Knocking her down the stairs was a tempting idea. But it was only an idea and I was a person. Ideas were a dime a dozen, and I wasn't going to tempt fate by faking being bad, because, who knew, maybe the part of me that was my own worst enemy, the old Joey, would like it if I was bad again and would keep me bad and I wouldn't get a second chance to be better. When I was little, I used to make a lot of ugly faces at everyone, and Grandma said to me once, 'If you keep that up, your face will stick that way.' And as soon as she said that, I started making a million ugly faces until my face hurt so much I wanted to stop, but I couldn't. I was so out of control, I kept sticking out my tongue and stretching my mouth with my fingers and pulling down my eyes and popping the skin off my eyelids and braying like a donkey and drooling down my chin and pulling stuff out of my nose. It was insane and painful, and by the time I wore myself out and went to sleep that night, my face was as sore as if someone had pinched me on it a million times. It was awful.

'No,' I said. 'I can't do it. It would be as if after being blind for a long time you got your eyesight back and it was beautiful and then suddenly I asked if you would be blind for a little while again to help me out – just for a little while – and then when I said so you could go back to seeing. Would you do that? I don't think so. And I wouldn't blame you.'

She looked at me for a moment as if she could see me. As if her eyesight had returned. At that moment I thought she understood everything I had just said, because I didn't think I could say it any better than I had.

'Well, I'm warning you,' she said sternly, 'if you won't be bad, I'll be even worse to you. I'll make your life unbearable!'

'You already are,' I said.

'I'm tired of you,' she snapped. 'Take me home. You can go looking for Pablo by yourself.'

'I'm going to look for him if it takes all night,' I said.

Suddenly she changed her tune. 'If you go at night, take me with you,' she said.

'No, I can't.'

'I've always wanted to go out at night,' she said.

'Will you tell my grandma you're my friend?'

'Never,' she replied, and crossed her arms across her chest.

I turned my back on her and began to tack up one last sign.

While I tapped away, she tiptoed out into the middle of the road, threw her cane into the air, and ran recklessly with her arms waving about and her head thrown back. 'Help!' she hollered as she ran. 'Joey Pigza is after me!'

'Stop!' I hollered, and ran after her. My sunglasses fell off, and my cane dropped to the street.

'Help!' she hollered. 'A maniac is trying to murder me!'

'That's not true!' I yelled as I passed a woman who was raking leaves. 'I'm a very nice boy!'

I was catching up to Olivia, but I didn't get to her in time. The road curved, and she went straight into the kerb and hit a fire hydrant with her leg and tumbled head over heels and landed on her face in the dirt, and by the time I got there I thought she was dead she was so stretched out.

Then she began to laugh. 'That was the best thing I've ever done,' she said, wiping dirt from her face.

'Let me see your leg,' I said. 'Did you hurt yourself?'

'Don't ruin the moment,' she said. 'I feel like I'm finally living dangerously.'

'No, you are making me live dangerously,' I replied, rubbing her leg. 'Your mom is going to kill me when she sees this bruise.'

I looked up at Olivia. She was smiling. 'Exactly,' she said.

Just then a squad car pulled up, and the very same cop that was at my door got out of his car. 'Hey,' he said. 'I saw you this morning. What's your name?'

'His name is Joey Pigza,' Olivia blurted out.

I gave her a pained look. Turning me in to the cops was about the meanest thing she could have done to me.

'Come on,' the cop said, and grabbed my wrist. 'I've been looking all over town for you. I need to take you down to the station.'

'Why? I didn't steal my own dog,' I cried.

'Your mother has taken out a restraining order against your dad, and we just need to have your fingerprints on file in case of an abduction,' he said. 'It's routine.'

'I wish you had Pablo's paw prints,' I said. 'He's the one who has been abducted.'

'Your friend better come along,' the cop said to me.

She's not my friend, I wanted to say as he helped her into the back seat with me.

When we arrived at the station the three of us went in. Olivia was smiling from ear to ear. 'Wait until my mom finds out about this,' she sang gleefully. 'I was hoping you would be a little bad to me, but being picked up by the cops is more than I ever could have hoped for.'

I dreaded what Mrs Lapp might say, but I didn't have time to think about it. The cop guided me over to a long table covered with equipment. 'Are your hands clean?' he asked.

I nodded. And then I just did what he told me to do. I didn't seem to have a choice. He took my hand and rolled my fingers one by one across a pad of sticky black ink, then rolled them again onto a special paper chart until he had all eight of my fingers and both my thumbs. And the whole time he was doing that, I was thinking the police were not really protecting me from my mom and dad as much as they were preparing to find me after something bad happened. And the only way something bad would happen was if either my mom or dad did something to hurt me. And in a way, at that moment, I didn't know who was hurting me more – my mom for not being with me when a cop was taking my fingerprints, or my dad for hounding us so that I had to get my finger-prints taken. Didn't she know this would scare me? Didn't he know he was scaring me? Didn't they know anything?

After the cop finished, he sent me to the bathroom to wash my hands. I stood in front of the sink with the water running over them and looked at myself in the mirror. I felt less safe instead of more safe. I looked down at my hands. The ink didn't come off with water, so I just rubbed them back and forth on the sides of my jeans until some of it came off and the rest of it just got pressed deeper into the lines on my hands so that they looked like rivers on maps of countries I had never seen before. I guess they no longer belonged to me now that they had been discovered by the police.

When I returned, Olivia was talking on the telephone with her mother. 'You'll never guess where we are. The police station! Joey is being fingerprinted because his mom is afraid his dad will steal him. Nobody would want to steal him. Even his dog was stolen before he was.'

She was right. Even Pablo was worth more than I was, although at that moment I felt smaller than him. I found a chair I could sit in and pulled my jacket up over my head. This was definitely bad thing number four, and I cried as quietly as I could. Olivia couldn't see my tears, and I didn't want her to hear them and feel good because I was feeling so bad.

Mrs Lapp picked us up at the police station. I got in her car and let Olivia do the talking. 'Don't you think we should kick Joey out of our school?' she said. 'He is so bad. He's like a criminal. I think he's a bad influence on me. I even feel *more* blind since he arrived.' She went on and on, and by the time we pulled up in front of my house, I just wanted to jump out the window and fly away, but Mrs Lapp turned in her seat and gave me a piercing look.

'I know this isn't your fault, Joey,' she said. 'It's your parents acting out. So don't worry about what Olivia is saying. I still want you in our school.' Then she leaned forward and whispered, 'You are still my secret helper.'

'Thanks,' I said, and half smiled.

'I don't want him back!' Olivia shouted.

'Hush,' Mrs Lapp said to her, and turned to me. 'I have something for Pablo.' She handed me a little silver medal the size of a penny. 'Read it,' she said eagerly.

On one side was stamped in large letters: D.O.G. On the other it read: DEPEND ON GOD. 'Thank you, Mrs Lapp,' I said. 'As soon as I find him, I'll put this on his collar.'

She smiled. 'I'm sure you'll find him,' she said. 'He's in our prayers. Right, Olivia?'

'No,' she said. 'He's a dog. I don't pray for dogs.'

I looked up at Mrs Lapp. 'Where do dogs go when they die?' I asked.

'Honey, they just die,' she said. 'They have no souls, so they stay in the ground.'

'Oh.' I said. I always thought all good pets went to heaven and all the bad ones went to that other place.

'Now go home and pray,' she said. 'God listens, and I'm sure he'll guide Pablo safely back to you.'

'Even if he doesn't have a soul?' I asked.

'God gave him legs,' she replied. 'And God always helps those who help themselves.'

That made me feel better because I knew in my heart that no matter where Pablo was, he was trying to get back to me.

7.
stockyards

That night when I saw the scratchy hand-writing on my LOST DOG sign in front of our house, I knew what had happened to Pablo. Dad had taken him. I ripped the paper down from the telephone pole. *Pablo loves me more*, it read. And it was signed, *Humpty Dumpty*. That was Dad's nickname. No one else in the world admired Humpty Dumpty as much as he did. 'All the king's horses and all the king's men couldn't put Humpty together again' is how he always made excuses for himself, as if he were something broken that could never be fixed. But he was wrong – someone always patched him back up. Mom told me she fixed him a zillion times, but he couldn't keep it together. His girlfriends tried with him, but he cracked up. People gave him jobs, but he messed them up. And when he got hurt, like when he was stuck on the tree, the doctors did a good job of sewing him back together. So I never thought he was a true Humpty Dumpty. The real Humpty wanted to be *together*. But Dad enjoyed being the most *un*together person I knew.

I crumpled the sign up in my hand and ran inside to check on Grandma and make sure she had some dinner. I sneaked up on her curtain and hollered out in my freak-show announcer voice, 'Ladies and gentle-men, I give you the one, the only zombie grandma from Lancaster!' And I yanked the curtain open.

She was sitting there hunched over and smoking a cigarette with a pained look on her face. She hadn't touched her envelopes. 'If I get any stiffer,' she said while rolling her neck around and stretching her fingers, 'you can prop me outside like a cigar store Indian.'

136

'Would you like something to eat?' I asked. She was getting so thin. Her shoulder blades looked like pterodactyl wings.

'Yes,' she said. 'I need some nourishment so I can write out my will.'

'Stop that!' I cried out.

'Believe me,' she said, 'when I'm dead, I'll be a lot easier to tend. You can just keep my ashes in a cigarette case and dust me off once a week.'

I ran into the kitchen and fixed her a cup of tea and lined the saucer with sugar biscuits. Most of her teeth were gone and she liked to dip the biscuits in and suck the tea out of them as they dissolved in her mouth.

When I brought it to her, she spotted my black fingertips. I told her about the cops picking me up. 'You know,' she said, 'I've had a lot of experience of washing off fingerprint ink. That's how I'd know if your dad had a wild night. I'd sneak into his room in the morning and check his hands. If they were inked up, I knew he had been up to something.'

'Well, he's up to something again,' I said. I uncrumbled the sign and handed it to her.

'That's his handwriting,' she confirmed.

'Do you think I should tell Mom?' I asked.

'No,' Grandma said. 'They got troubles of their own. She called last night after you were asleep and said she and Booth were going to hide out at a motel because your dad was bugging them.'

'Which motel?' I asked.

'She didn't know yet,' Grandma replied. 'Said she'd call back.'

'Well, why do you think he took Pablo?' I asked.

'Only he can tell you that,' she said. 'No one can read that man's mind.'

'I think he's at the stockyards,' I said. 'That's where I saw him going the other night.'

'That sounds about right,' she said. 'He's more animal than man.'

And then, right when we were talking about him, I thought I could hear Dad's motorcycle cutting through the cemetery behind the house. I ran to the back window and saw his single light skipping across the tombstones. Now that he had taken Pablo, I finally understood why Mom was furious with him when he first started buzzing us. She knew he was nothing but trouble, because once he arrived, he didn't stop being trouble until he had messed everything up and there was nothing more for him to ruin. And now that she was hiding out with Booth, he became my trouble. Once I heard him turn the corner I ran outside. In a minute he roared up our street, and as he did so, I pulled off my jacket and waved it around in the air over my head. Unlike Mom, I didn't want to kill him. I just wanted to talk. But he didn't. Just before he roared by, he reached back into his saddlebag, then stuck out his leather gloved hand. He was holding Pablo by the belly, and Pablo's eyes were all bugged out, and his little front legs were stretched forward as if he were Super Dog flying through the air.

'Pablo!' I yelled. 'Pablo!'

But Dad kept going.

'At least get him a helmet!' I yelled as loud as I could.

He sped up Plum Street, and the noise from his motorcycle was like a giant finger that pointed out exactly where he was heading. I could hear him pass the ice factory, then go under the railroad bridge, up the hill past the Goodwill box, beyond the

All-American Discount Grocery Store, and back into the stockyards, where he had gone the other night. That's where he was hiding. Now Pablo was there. And I was going to have to go there too.

I took a deep breath and started running after him. I made it to the parking lot at the grocery store when a police car pulled up behind me. Not again, I thought, and shoved my fists into my pockets. But it was a different policeman.

'What are you doing here?' the cop asked.

'Searching for my lost dog,' I said.

'Are you sure you aren't trying to buy some liquor?' he asked harshly. 'Because I'm searching for a guy who's been buying liquor for kids. Have you seen anyone around here?'

'No,' I said. 'My dog ran up this way, and I've come to find him.'

'Well, if you see a strange man selling liquor, give us a call at the station.'

'There's a scary guy who sometimes sleeps under the railroad bridge,' I said.

'I know,' he said, 'but he's OK.' Then he pulled away.

Once he was out of sight, I entered the

gate of the old stockyard. As I walked between the rows of empty cow pens the feeling of belonging nowhere was everywhere. It was creepy. I think it was because all the cows were gone and the only things left were the old, warped fence boards that used to corral them. Instead of wood, the boards looked like a graveyard of ribs. Even though I lived next to a cemetery, the stockyard felt more lifeless. People still cared about their dead relatives and put flowers on the graves. But no one cared about the stockyards. The only things left behind were so worthless they would soon rot down to nothing. But somewhere in there I knew Dad was hiding. And I knew he had the dogs. After he had passed me, I listened for his motorcycle, and it had stopped. He didn't make it to the highway on the other side of the stockyard. He was hiding in the middle. I had to find him if I wanted Pablo, so I stood still and listened. Slowly I turned my head one way, then the other, like Olivia. And I thought I could hear yapping. So I zigzagged deeper into the maze, stepping over some boards, ducking under others, and the deeper I went, the more I was certain I heard barking. And then, against the starry night sky, I could make out the darker outline of a tiny shack and a yellow light winking out of a crack in a boarded-up window.

I sneaked up to the shack and pushed my eye against the crack, as if I were looking through a telescope. The small room was brightly lit by a kerosene lamp. There was Dad sitting on the floor with six yapping Chihuahuas bouncing off him like furry springs, snapping at him, tugging on his leathers, and biting his ears. He was a busier dognapper than I thought. He was laughing and throwing a red rubber ball around the small room that all six of them would chase after and fight each other for to be the one to take it back to Dad, who put it between his teeth like a pig with an apple cooked in his mouth while the dogs tugged on the ball, tearing away little red pieces of it.

I guess because it all seemed so funny to me, I wasn't as scared as I normally would have been, and I rapped my knuckles on the boarded-up window. 'Hello!' I shouted. The dogs went into an insane frenzy of barking, and Dad jumped up and ran out the front door, and in two seconds he had me pinned down on the ground with his face an inch above mine.

'You're hurting me!' I cried.

'You surprised me,' he replied, pulling his hands from my shoulders. 'I thought you were one of those wild Amish kids coming around here to get me in more trouble. They told the cops I bought them some beer, and now the cops are trying to run me out of town.'

'Well, the cops took me to the police station today,' I said.

'What'd you do?' he asked, smiling, as if going to the police station was something to be proud of.

'Nothing,' I said as he gave me a hand up. 'I just have two parents who are fighting over me, and the cops wanted my finger-prints in case I'm abducted.'

'Don't worry,' Dad said. 'I won't abduct you.'

'You abducted Pablo,' I said.

'That's only because I wanted to talk with you,' he replied. 'It was the only way I could think to have you come here.'

'Why didn't you just come get me?' I asked. 'Or use the phone?'

'You know your mom doesn't want me around, so I had to be a bit sneaky. And now she has a restraining order out against me. I'm not allowed to call you, or be around you or her in any way.'

'There's nothing sneaky about taking every Chihuahua in town,' I pointed out.

He laughed. 'They all look the same to me,' he said. 'Besides, if I snatch a dog off the street, nobody will care. But if I snatch you, then I'm kidnapping, and I'm locked up for the rest of my life. And as much as I wanted to see you, this way *you* have really come to see me.'

'Well, what do you want from me?' I asked.

'I want to know something for sure,' he said.

'What?'

'I want to know if your mom and you ever want me back, or if you are always going to think I'm a total knucklehead and never want to see me again.'

'She already has a boyfriend she's thinking of marrying,' I said.

'She may want to be with that Booth guy, but I've been watching him around town. He's just some clown with a camera.'

'And Mom thinks you're just some clown with a motorcycle,' I said. 'If you were nice to her, she might be nice back.'

'True,' he agreed. And then he smiled his evil biker smile. 'But then I'd have to be nice to her, then she'd be nice to me, and we would just be like some seesaw of niceness going up and down.'

'Yeah,' I said. 'What's wrong with that?'

'I've never been able to stay long on the seesaw,' he said. 'As soon as I get the other person up in the air, I hop off and *ka-boom!* They crash to the ground.'

'Didn't anyone show you how to play nice?' I asked.

'Yeah. But you may have noticed I'm a bit of a loser. It's not that I don't know how to play nice, it's that I don't want to play nice. That's the difference.'

'I know a kid who thinks just the way you do,' I said.

'You mean that girl I see you with?'

'Yeah,' I said. 'She's always getting me in trouble or hurting my feelings or something bad.'

'Only a sucker would put up with a friend like that,' he said.

'Well, do you think I'm a sucker?' I asked.

He paused. 'Not really,' he replied. 'I'm the sucker. I wouldn't have the patience to put up with someone like that, so I'd never stick around long enough to find out if they would ever learn how to be nice.'

'And do you think we should put up with you long enough to find out if you will ever be nice?'

He ran his hand over his chin and rubbed the sore spot where Mom had kicked him. 'That's a good question,' he said. 'No amount of goodness seems to improve me. I just get worse to everyone, including myself.'

'But you wanted to see me,' I said, 'so you must still be trying to do something right.'

He took a cigarette out of his pack and offered me one.

'I don't smoke,' I said.

'I did when I was your age,' he boasted, then shrugged his shoulders as he lit up. 'There's only a few things I can do with my life,' he said, exhaling loudly. 'I can smoke, which I do. I can drink, which I do. And I can chase after your mom every blue moon, which I do. And right now I'm under the spell of a blue moon.'

'But why?' I asked.

'Because from time to time I think that if I was back with her, she'd help me get a grip on myself.'

'And then what?'

'And then after a while I'd get mad at her for not allowing me to screw my life up. You know, it's a vicious cycle. And right now I'm at the part of the cycle where I want your mom back.'

'Well, that's news to me,' I said. 'The only thing you've done so far is scare us half to death. And now you stole Pablo.'

'That's part of the cycle too,' he said. 'I want you back, but then when I have you, it drives me loco to have to be responsible all the time.'

'Then maybe you shouldn't want us,' I said. 'Maybe you should leave us alone.'

'You could be right, son. Besides, I'm tired of camping out here,' he said, waving towards the stockyard. 'It's depressing. Yet I don't have a clue about what I should do next.'

'Get some help,' I urged.

'I've tried that,' he replied. 'Help just means that someone tells me I've got to

147

start making good decisions for myself.'

'Yeah,' I said. 'That's exactly what help is.'

'What fun is there in that?' he asked, and grinned, as if he were thinking of something bad he'd rather do, like get drunk or do something to drive Mom crazy. 'Help is just something you think about while you're busy having fun, and fun is what you're doing while help takes its time finding you.'

'That doesn't sound right to me,' I said. 'When I'm having fun, I'm not thinking of help. I'm just hoping the fun never stops.'

'I told you,' he said, and winked at me. 'I'm wired backward.'

He took a drag off his cigarette, and I could see his fingers shaking.

'Are you sad?' I asked.

He took another shaky drag, then tried to laugh, but it wasn't a laugh. He was sad, and the laugh was like crying in reverse. 'I just need a drink is all,' he replied. 'Pity I can't be happy with my own sadness. But the bottle has got me trapped inside it like one of those little ships you can't shake out and the only way you can get it out is to break the whole thing.' He looked up at me.

'You've got your med patch to keep you steady,' he said. 'Well, I need a Fran patch to keep me steady. I need your help getting her back,' he said, finally getting to the point.

I didn't know what to say to that.

'You sure you don't want a cigarette?' Dad asked, lighting a fresh one off the old one.

I almost said yes because I was so relieved to change the subject. But I said, 'No.' Suddenly I heard a loud cow snort. 'I thought this place was empty.' I remarked.

'Not entirely,' he said. 'There's still some meat-on-feet.' He pointed out at the stockyard. 'Mostly old good-for-nothing bulls,' he said. 'We're living the loser life together. Next week they'll be chopped meat, and I'll be chopped liver.'

'It's getting late, Dad,' I said. 'Can I see the dogs?'

'Sure.' He opened the door, and they all came running out like a miniature stampede of cattle.

'Pablo!' I shouted, and dropped down to my knees. He ran into my arms.

'Rat-dogs is what they are,' Dad remarked, and scooped up a handful of dirt and threw it at them. They began barking like a string of firecrackers. 'A real man would have a dog like a Dobermann, or a German shepherd or a pit bull – not some girlie dog that fits in a purse.

'He's not a cissy dog,' I said. 'He's not afraid of anything. Me, or you, or even that old bull.' I stood up and went over to the shadowy pen with the bull.

'Get 'em, killer,' I ordered, and set Pablo on the ground. Pablo ran straight at him, yapping all the way. The bull couldn't have cared less. It stood looking at me with eyes as dark and shiny as black billiard balls while Pablo snipped and snapped at its hoof trying to get the bull to do something. Finally Pablo leaped up and bit the bull on a clump of matted fur and mud. He hung on there, growling. The bull looked away and took a deep breath.

'OK,' Dad agreed. 'Pablo is no cissy dog. But who is man enough to pull Pablo off the bull?'

'I'll do it,' I said.

I snapped my fingers. Pablo opened his jaws and fell to the ground. He popped up onto his feet and ran towards me.

'You win,' Dad said. 'He's a real killer. And you are his master. Now, come on,' he said. 'I'll put these dogs in a sack, and I'll give you a ride home.'

'First we have to stop by the hospital,' I said. 'They have some medicine waiting for you,'

'Oh yeah, that's right,' he said, remembering as he rubbed his side with his hand. 'I'll do that later. Let me get you home first.' He went inside the shack and came out with a feed sack. I picked up the dogs one by one and set them in. They wriggled around like cats about to be drowned.

He put the sack in his saddlebag and lifted me onto the back seat. 'Hang onto my shoulders,' he said. 'It's a bumpy ride getting out of here.'

He started the motorcycle, and we took off, and I grabbed him around the neck. he knew his way through the maze of pens, and before long we were roaring down Plum Street past the grocery store and under the railroad bridge, and then he veered off and instead of going to the front of our house, he turned down Maple Avenue and slowed down and pulled into St Mary's Cemetery.

After he picked up a little speed, he cut off the engine, and we glided down the narrow asphalt path and pulled up at the back of our house.

'You know,' Dad said, 'I've been thinkin' just now. I see how well you are doing, and I want to be well too. I think you gave me some help tonight.'

'Thanks,' I said, feeling so proud of myself for what he said.

'I'll try harder with Fran,' he said. 'By the way, do you know where she's hiding out?'

'Dad, don't be scary,' I replied.

'I'll try,' he said.

'I hope so,' I said. 'Because if you were nice, it wouldn't be so bad to have you around here.'

'You mean that, son?' he asked.

'I do,' I replied.

'Hey, those two words are what people say when they get married. *I do*. I remember them well. Does she ever talk about the good times we had together?'

'Dad,' I said, 'I've got to go now. I have a lot of dogs to take care of and your mom too.'

'Goodnight,' he said, and reached around and gave me a hug, and I hugged him back.

'One question,' I asked. 'What happened to your last girlfriend? She was nice.'

'The same thing that happened to you,' he replied. 'She got to know me too well.' He grinned, then started the motorcycle, and whatever else he had to say was silenced behind the sound of that engine.

And there I was, standing with a sack full of growling Chihuahuas, in a cemetery, thinking that now I was Mom's helper, and Mrs Lapp's helper, and Olivia's helper, and Grandma's helper, and Dad's helper, and Pablo's helper, and the helper for a sackful of unhappy dogs. I didn't know if that was a good thing or a bad thing. I knew Grandma would say I should just help myself and let the others figure it out for themselves, but I couldn't let them down. So I lifted the sack up over the cemetery fence and into my backyard. It was time to get them sorted out and ready for bed. I figured I'd return them in the morning.

8

Day by Day

I had left the dogs in the bathroom all night. In the morning I got a piece of clothesline rope and one by one tied them all to me, and when I was finished they looked like a Chihuahua charm bracelet that had fallen off a giant lady. They were yapping and straining in all different directions with their hard nails scratching at the wooden floor while Pablo ran a circle around us and snipped and snapped at them and stirred up trouble. I looked at him and shook my finger back and forth. Pablo had only been with Dad for a short while, but he was already acting just like him – *sinking to his level*.

'Pablo Pigza!' I shouted above all the noise. 'You better straighten up, or you are headed for a time-out.'

He took off through the house barking and yapping as if he were on a tiny circus motorcycle driving crazily between the furniture.

'I'll deal with you later, young man,' I shouted as he scrambled around a chair. 'Right now I've got a job to do.' I looped my end of the rope around a doorknob and went into the bathroom. It was a swampy mess. I backed out and went to the kitchen, where I got a roll of paper towels, then returned and wiped everything up. Since we didn't have air freshener, I sprayed some old cologne around. It was brownish and smelled like rotting leaves, which was perfect since Thanksgiving was just around the corner.

'I'll be back in a little bit,' I hollered to Grandma. 'Anything I can get you while I'm out?' I knew she was still alive because I could see smoke rising above her curtain, and I could hear the dry sound of paper being folded.

'A friend,' she croaked.

'Can I get back to you on that?' I hollered, and I opened our front door and all the Chihuahuas went insane and scrambled through and across the porch. I slammed the door, and we went spinning around like the Mad Hatter's teacups with all of them tipping over and falling down the stairs and me behind them. Once we hit the sidewalk, I took off running, and they took off after me. I sang out, 'Rolling, rolling, rolling! Keep them doggies rolling, rawww-hide!' And they rolled along – tripping, tumbling, yapping like a band of scuffed-up mariachis.

When I arrived at the Lapps' house I rang the doorbell.

Mrs Lapp answered. 'W.W.J.D.?' she chimed as always. Then she looked down at all the dogs and took a step back as if I had a gang of rabid rats with me. 'Oh, my!' she exclaimed, and her eyes got very big.

'I have to return these lost dogs to their proper homes,' I replied as quickly as I could. 'My dad stole them by mistake, and I'm helping him out.'

'Good idea,' she said, relieved. 'Because you can't bring them all in here.'

'What's going on?' Olivia shouted from the

156

living room as she marched across the carpet.

'My Dad had all the Chihuahuas, and after I found him, he gave them to me, and now I have to return them,' I shouted, as if she were deaf too.

Mrs Lapp cupped her hands around her mouth and leaned forward. 'Invite her along,' she whispered into my ear. 'She needs to get out some. She's been a little terror this morning already.'

I didn't want to. But I didn't have a choice.

'Do you want to come with me on a really long, dangerous, stinky, awful chore?' I droned, like a dying bagpipe.

'The nastier the better,' Olivia replied. I looked down at her leg. She had her pant leg rolled up and a big seeping bandage below her knee.

'When you return, we'll do a Bible lesson on all of this,' Mrs Lapp offered.

'Jesus and the Chihuahuas?' I asked. I had never heard of that before.

'No, lost lambs,' she said, and patted me on the head as if I were a lost Joey.

I had already looked at all the dog tags and made up a route for returning them.

'This one is from Lime Street,' I said when Olivia was suited up with her walking gear. 'Let's go.'

'You be careful,' Mrs Lapp advised, and pointed to Olivia's leg.

'Don't worry,' I replied. 'I've got a posse of Chihuahuas to protect us.'

'And I'm the baddest blind girl in town,' Olivia said, slashing the air with her cane so wildly that I had to duck.

We were a weird team. She tapped and the dogs yapped and we zigzagged our way down the street like the drunks stumbling around the bus station.

When we arrived at the red brick house on Lime Street, a little old man wearing a plaid golf cap and stained T-shirt answered the door. 'Yes?' he asked.

'I think my dad stole your dog,' I said. 'Baxter?'

He smiled and covered his heart with his hands. 'Where? Where?' he cried joyously, before suddenly staring down at the five Chihuahuas and trying to figure out which was his. 'Baxter! Baxter!'

Baxter jumped into his lowered arms, and I untied the leash from my wrist and backed out of the doorway. Olivia and I and the other four Chihuahuas continued to scratch, tap, and yap our way down the sidewalk.

'He didn't even give you a reward,' Olivia said.

'I don't want a reward,' I replied. 'My dad *stole* the dogs, and I'm doing this because it's the right thing to do.'

'You are such a sucker,' she said.

'Am not,' I snapped back. 'I'm just trying to help.'

'Sucker,' she insisted.

'Am not,' I muttered.

'Are too,' she whispered.

Am not, I said to myself with my lips barely buzzing.

The next owner was on the shady side of King Street. An old lady in a house dress came to the Dutch door. I gave little Charro back to her. She held her dog up to her face and kissed her right on the lips. 'I knew if I made ice cream you'd come home,' she said in a baby voice, and squeezed Charro's skinny belly. 'So that's just what I was doing.'

I grinned.

'And what is your name, young man?'

'You can just call me Mr Helpful,' I said and blushed. 'And you can call her the Mistress of All Evil.'

Once Olivia heard that, she snapped to attention. She tucked her chin into her chest and glowered at the woman with her large cloudy eyes. It was frightening.

The lady held Charro to her chest. 'OK, Mr Helpful,' she said, smiling at me, 'and Mistress Evil,' she said hesitantly. 'I'll make you a batch of ice cream. Can I bring some to you?'

I gave her my address. 'We're having a family get-together on Thanksgiving,' I said. 'Stop by because we include anyone nice in our family.'

'I won't be there,' Olivia growled.

The lady looked at me. I held my finger to my lips and shrugged. There really was no explanation for Olivia's bad attitude.

I looked at the next dog tag. The address was on Prince Street.

As we walked in front of the Fulton Opera House, there were big signs advertising *Godspell*, and overhead 'Day by Day' was playing on a tinny speaker.

'That's *Godspell*!' Olivia said suddenly,

turning her ear towards the speakers. 'Are we at the opera house?'

'Yes,' I said, though I had never been inside it before.

'I heard on the radio that *Godspell* is playing, and I have to go,' she announced.

'Then go,' I said.

'My mom doesn't approve of it. She thinks Bible musicals are bad because they turn religion into entertainment.'

I didn't know what to say to that because mostly my mind was still thinking about what she had just said – that she'd like to go. I think it was the first positive thing she had ever said she wanted to do. I don't remember her saying that she even *wanted* to have eyesight.

Suddenly all that talk about having to 'go' made me have to *go*. I began hopping back and forth as if I were dodging bullets. I tried to open the opera house door, but it was locked. 'I'll be right back,' I said. 'I gotta go to the bathroom. But watch out,' I warned her. 'My dad is still around and he's insane, and I told him you were mean to me, and if he catches you with the dogs, there's no telling what he'll do.'

'Don't worry about me,' she replied, and raked her cane across the sidewalk hard enough to make sparks. 'I can handle him.'

I put all the leashes around her wrist and ran across the street. Then I stopped and checked on her. She stood there singing 'Day by Day' out loud, twisting back and forth and bobbing up and down like a lost ship on the ocean. She kept all her happiness to herself, I thought, and never shared it with me.

After I did what I needed to do behind a bush, I got an idea. I thought I'd give her a taste of her own medicine and scare her inside out and see just how much she liked it when someone was mean to her. I took off running and at the end of the block turned left and after that another left and another left until I had circled back to her, and then when I was a block away, I stopped and began to tiptoe forward so that soon I was standing in her shadow, which was right behind her, as if I were a ghoul hiding in the forest, and then before the dogs even noticed me, I leaped forward and yelled, 'BOO!' and grabbed her shoulders. She shrieked out loud as if I had stabbed her. She dropped her cane, and it clattered across the brick sidewalk. Her legs buckled, and she crumpled down in a heap, and the dogs began barking.

I didn't know what to do. 'Olivia!' I said desperately as I dropped to my knees. 'Are you OK?'

She moaned.

'Olivia?'

Her cloudy eyes rolled towards mine. 'You are in so much trouble,' she said angrily. 'I almost had a heart attack. I almost died.'

'I'm sorry,' I said, panting because I was so scared. 'It was kind of a joke, but I guess it wasn't funny.'

'You guessed right,' she snapped.

'I'm sorry,' I said. 'Really sorry.' I tried to help her up, but she pushed me aside and got up on her own. She bent down and ran her hands across the bricks until she located her cane. And as we started up the street, I pranced around her and said about a million times. 'Sorry, soooooo sorry.' And I was so nervous because I had done something wrong. I sneaked up and scared a blind girl. What was I thinking? The only person in the world who would think this was a good idea was Dad. Now I was following in his footsteps.

Olivia didn't say anything no matter how many times I said sorry, so we continued up Prince Street until we came to a small wooden house where one of the dogs lived. I knocked on a door. No one answered. But there was a little rubber doggy door flap, and as I stood there, the dog went right in, and I knew it was his home. I wished it was my home because at that moment I wanted to crawl through a doggy door and curl up in a corner and hide. But I couldn't fit. I untied his leash from around my wrist and figured his owners would find a happy surprise when they got home.

'If you were really sorry for being so awful to me,' she said as I planned how to return the next pet, 'you would sneak me out of my house and take me to *Godspell*.'

'I can't do that,' I said. 'Your mom would kill me.'

'Well, what if I kill you first?' she said bitterly, then sneered at where she thought I was standing but missed me.

'Help yourself,' I replied.

'You *could* help me,' she said. 'I'd unplug

164

the little door monitor, and then you could sneak me out.'

'And how would I get tickets?' I asked, remembering a sign in the ticket-booth window. 'They are forty-five dollars each.'

'W.W.J.D.?' she replied. 'Where there's a will, there's a way.'

'I'm not stealing money,' I said.

'Get it from your dad,' she suggested.

'He's broke,' I said.

'Your mom?'

'She's broke too.'

'Your grandma?'

'That's her lung money,' I replied. 'We can't use that.'

'Well, if you helped me, I might be willing to help you do something,' she offered.

'Are you trying to make a deal?' I asked.

'Perhaps,' she said.

I though for a moment. 'Would you visit my grandma?'

She didn't say anything, which was almost like saying yes.

'Really, it would be a good thing to do,' I said. 'Because then she could die in peace knowing I had a friend.'

'That sounds crazy to me.'

'No, really, that's what she told me. That she "can't die in peace" until she is certain I can make a friend, because I've never had one.'

'Are you saying if I tell her we're friends, she'll drop dead?' she asked.

'Well, that's what she says,' I said, 'but I don't believe her.'

'Then let's call her bluff,' Olivia said, eagerly. 'Maybe she'll keel over at our feet. Now that would be something.'

'She's not *really* going to die,' I said. 'She's just going to stop worrying about me and start feeling better.' But Olivia wasn't listening.

'Do you think when I say the word *friend* that she'll clutch her heart and hit the floor? Or fall backwards? Or have a stroke and go down in a heap?'

'Stop it,' I said. 'That's really sick.'

'OK,' she groaned. 'I'll make a deal with you. I'll visit your grandma and tell her I am your blind-as-a-bat friend and send her to her grave, if you help me sneak out of my house and take me to the opera. How's that?'

'Give me some time to think about it,' I said.

'I'll check back with you in a minute,' she said. 'But I'm warning you, I'm not going to wait all day.'

'OK,' I said. 'OK.'

We walked silently all the way across St James Street until we found the next house and scuffed through the fallen leaves in the yard as we headed for the front door. I rang the bell.

A very old lumpy person opened the door with something like a Christmas stocking on their head and I couldn't tell if it was a man or a woman or one of my little gnome friends come to life. There were some long whiskers on the chin, but that didn't mean anything because my grandma has whiskers on hers. The person wore pants, but my grandma wore pants. The person had short hair sticking out, but my grandma had short hair. 'Can I help you?' the person asked, as if Olivia and I were lost.

'I'm returning Little Bit,' I said.

The person looked down at Little Bit and seemed very disappointed.

'Goodness,' the person said slowly. 'I thought I'd never see LB again, and we already went out and got another dog – a German shepherd puppy – and I don't think they'll mix too well.'

'Well, Little Bit is yours,' I said.

'He was my son's,' the person said. 'But he moved out of the basement and left the dog with us. Maybe you can just take him to the pound?'

I felt bad for Little Bit, who looked up at the person and whimpered. Then the German shepherd puppy came to the door and began to bark, so we backed away. When I reached the sidewalk, I stooped down to scratch Little Bit's ears. 'Can you believe that,' I said to her. 'She doesn't want you any more, which means you are *mine*.' And it occurred to me that I had just made a friend for Pablo. Even though he never told me he wanted a friend, I figured he must want someone his size in the house. After all, his neck must constantly be sore from always having to look way up at everything in the world.

The last dog didn't have a collar but I figured it was Rita from the Dogs Missing section of the paper. We took it to the Lancaster Pet Centre and after I explained my story again about my dad, the animal nurse took a look at the Chihuahua and said she could probably figure out where it lived since they usually took care of most all the dogs in town or knew enough people, and some of them would know who was missing a Chihuahua.

When we got to my house, Olivia turned to me. 'Times up,' she said. 'What's it going to be?'

'Are you sure you can pull the plug on the door guard?' I asked.

'Sure,' she said.

'OK,' I said reluctantly. 'I'll swap. You come into my house now, and I'll get you out of yours later.'

'Deal,' she said, and stuck out her hand.

I shook it. It was very soft, like shaking a velvet glove.

'Sit here a minute,' I said. 'I'll be right back.'

I grabbed Little Bit and ran up the steps and into the house. 'Pablo!' I hollered. 'Pablo! Come here.' When he arrived, he peered up at me and began sniffing. He seemed confused. 'What do you think of this?' I said, bending down and standing the new Chihuahua on the floor.

'See, now you have a friend,' I said to Pablo, 'and you won't strain your neck. We'll name her Pablita.'

While they were sniffing each other and getting reacquainted, I called out, 'Grandma?'

'Still breathing,' she called back, as if she were stuck down a well.

'I got a surprise for you,' I sang out. 'On the front steps.'

'Give me a minute to clean up,' she hollered.

I went back outside. 'One more minute,' I said. 'Then you can come in.'

'I don't know,' she said, standing up. 'Let me think about this some more.'

'Come on,' I said impatiently, and reached for her hand, 'we made a deal.'

But she wasn't fighting me too hard, otherwise she would have smacked me with her cane.

'OK,' she said.

'Follow me,' I said. She tapped up the steps as I scampered in front of her and opened the door. 'Watch out for the opening,' I said. 'There's a little half-step.'

'Hush,' she whispered. 'Don't tell me what to do.'

'I just don't want you to fall flat on your face.'

'That'll be your grandma's job,' she cracked with a wicked smile.

'You be nice,' I shot right back.

She grinned as she tapped her way across the living room until her stick hit the shower curtain. 'What's this?' she asked.

I didn't say. I just went into my circus ringmaster voice. 'Ladies and gentlemen,' I shouted. 'I give you the *one*, the *only*, Granny Pigza! Tougher than whip leather. And true predictor of the future.' I yanked open the curtain.

Grandma was sitting there smoking a cigarette. She had on orange lipstick and an ironed Hawaiian shirt, which was good because her skin was so grey, she looked like frozen smoke. 'Nice to meet you, young lady,' she rasped, and flicked the ashes into her hand.

Olivia lifted her cane and tapped Grandma's legs.

'Stop hitting me,' Grandma ordered. 'Don't

you have any manners? I'm a person, not a street kerb.'

Olivia's shoulders slumped down.

'Joey,' Grandma asked, 'does she talk?'

I turned to Olivia. 'Tell her who you are,' I whispered. 'You know.'

'I'm Olivia. Joey's *friend*,' she spat out as if she were flinging a knife at a tree stump. Then she paused as if she were waiting for Grandma to gasp, keel over, and hit the floor with a thud.

'I'm his grandmother, and I'm really pleased to meet you,' Grandma said, and stuck out her hand to shake, but then thought better of it and pulled it back. Then she turned to me. 'Well, Joey, you did the impossible. I have to give you credit. You made a friend who can't possibly *see* what a certified nut you are.'

'I know,' I said proudly with my chest all pumped out. 'Good choice, don't you think?'

'She never saw you coming,' Grandma said, and then cracked herself up and fell into a coughing fit that nearly killed her.

'Can I sit down?' Olivia asked.

'Sure you can,' Grandma said, choking on her words. 'Would you like a cigarette?'

'Yes,' Olivia replied, and smiled.

'Well, you can't have one 'cause they'll kill you.' Grandma said, and again fell into a laughing and coughing fit.

'Sometimes I think dying is not such a bad idea,' Olivia said.

'If being blind was any reason to kill myself,' Grandma replied, 'I would have done so years ago when I was blinded.'

Blinded? I had never heard that before. Somehow just hearing Grandma say 'blinded' got me moving around like I had ants in my pants. I didn't want her to get Olivia all riled up and have her take back that she was my friend. I ran into the kitchen and put the tea kettle on. I could still listen from there.

'What happened?' Olivia asked after a few moments.

'I was milking a cow when I was a girl and got kicked between the eyes. It knocked me stone cold, and I was in a coma for three days. When I came out of it, I was blind as midnight. Stayed that way for three weeks, and the whole time I was convinced that I was blinded for life, and I prayed like the worst sinner ever, and before you know it my

173

sight came back. The doctor said it just took time for my optical nerve to heal. But I figured it was the praying that done it.'

'That's an inspiring story,' Olivia said flatly as I swooped through the living room yelling, 'Can I fix anyone some tea?' as if I were a waiter on roller skates. Olivia and Grandma both ignored me.

'Too bad I wasn't just kicked in the head,' Olivia said.

'That can be arranged,' Grandma replied. 'When I got my sight back, I kicked that cow in the head and just about blinded her.' She laughed out and stomped her foot on the floor, and I about jumped up to the ceiling I was so nervous.

Olivia smiled.

'I got a lot of stories,' Grandma announced. 'My daddy went blind once from drinking some home-made corn liquor. Took him a week to get his sight back. Then there was the time my aunt was on the house fixing the weathervane, and she was hit by lightning, which left her blind for the better part of a year. And Joey's dad went blind once from cracking walnuts with his forehead. But his sight returned. His brain didn't, but that's a whole 'nother story.'

'You know how I went blind?' Olivia asked.

Her words were like a strong magnet. I leaned so far forward, I almost tripped over. I had always wanted to know but never had the guts to ask.

'Tell me, girl,' Grandma said.

'My mother was bit by a snake when she was pregnant with me. She and my father were at a church retreat, and one of her earrings fell off when they were walking over some rocks. It fell into a crack, and when she reached down, there was a rattlesnake coiled inside and it bit her. Her hand swelled up real bad, and they rushed her to the hospital, but because she was pregnant they couldn't give her the anti-venom, and she had to wait it out. Then when I was born I was blind, and that's why my mother is so upset all the time because she knows I was blinded by a snake – and to her that means I've been blinded by the devil, which makes me *possessed*.'

'Really?' Grandma remarked. 'You mean to tell me that you are blaming your bad behaviour on being possessed? Why, that's a good one. Joey's wired, but I can't blame the devil for it.'

'Mom says Joey is possessed,' Olivia said. 'Says the devil has a pitchfork to his back-side all day long.'

Grandma looked at me. 'Well, that might explain it,' she said, then slapped her knee and began to cough instead of laugh. 'Why don't you and your mom come over for dessert on Thanksgiving, and we can swap opinions about you two rascals?'

'Sounds good to me,' Olivia said, standing up. 'My dad's on the road but I'll tell my mom. I think she'd like to hear some of your opinions. Probably peel her skin back.'

Grandma laughed. 'I have a reputation for that,' she said, bragging.

'I just have one question,' Olivia asked. 'Why do you want him to have a friend so badly?'

'Because it would have made a difference for me,' she said directly. 'If I'd had a few friends around to help me out, I'd have done things differently in my life – done a few things better – like raise him right.' She pointed at me as if I were some kind of freak.

'But what if they are bad friends?' she asked.

'Then they are just bad people,' Grandma said. 'Good friends will stick with you no matter what.'

Olivia didn't say anything. She stood there for a minute thinking about what Grandma said. The tapping of her cane against the heel of her shoe sounded like an idling engine. Finally she said, 'We'll bake pies and bring them down on Thanksgiving.' Then she spun around and for a moment rotated her face back and forth like a radar antenna, then tapped her way directly towards the front door. I ran over and flung it open before she hit the glass panel. She went out to the porch, and I dashed back to Grandma. Just because I made a friend, I didn't want her to think it was OK to drop dead.

'Don't worry,' she replied, as if reading my thoughts. She took a long pull on her oxygen tube and cracked her knuckles. 'I feel better than I have in years.'

Suddenly Olivia screamed, and I heard her tumble down the stairs. When I got there, she was spread out on the sidewalk like a crumpled X.

'Don't say a word,' she warned me.

I didn't. I just helped her up and put her cane in her hands. Now she had hurt her other leg.

'You know,' she said as I guided her back to the steps, 'you are bad luck!'

'Well, I don't know what you are,' I said, 'except that you're mean as a snake to me and I wish I knew why.'

Suddenly the teakettle whistled. I had forgotten all about it.

'Hold on,' I said, and jumped up. I went inside and turned off the heat, and when I came back out, I sat beside her. Olivia had an expression on her face that I'd never seen before.

She reached out and held my arm. 'Joey, you're so blind you can't see this has nothing to do with you. It's all about *me*. You are the umpteenth kid my mom has lured in to be my home-schooling partner, but I've chased them all off. Last year we went through all the home-school kids from church. Mom said you are my last chance, and after you go, they'll send me to a Christian boarding school for blind kids, which will be great for me because I'll finally be treated like a regular kid instead of some invalid.'

I just stared at her. I felt so dumb. I thought people were mean because they couldn't help it. I never would have guessed being mean to me was some kind of sneaky plan.

'Joey, I want you to tell my mom you're giving up on me,' she said. 'That you won't be her "secret helper" any more.'

I stood there looking down at my feet.

'I'm asking you to help me with my problem. Will you or won't you?' she asked.

'But I already told your mom I would help you be nice.'

'Well, I am nice,' she said. 'Don't you agree?'

'Can I get back to you on that?' I whispered.

'Take your time, Einstein,' she whispered back, then reached around for her cane, which was bent up like a lightning bolt.

When we got to her house, I was exhausted. It wasn't that the walk was long. But it seemed that I was thinking ten times harder than I ever had, which made the walk feel ten times longer.

'Is your leg OK?' I asked before she limped inside and I had to tell Mrs Lapp what had happened.

She nodded. 'By the way,' she said, 'you were right. Your grandmother is like me. She tells it like it is.'

'I said you two had a lot in common.'

'I hope I didn't kill her,' she replied. 'I mean that.'

'Don't worry,' I said, and patted her on the shoulder. 'She's tough as nails. If she was going to die, I would have done her in years ago.'

9
Haircut

After school Grandma was waiting for me. She was sorting out her bits and pieces of plastic jewellery, which she kept in her old cigar box. 'I can't believe you did it,' she rasped. 'You made a friend.'

'I hardly did anything,' I replied. 'You did all the talking. That blind story you told really won her over. Especially the praying part.'

'I made that whole thing up,' she said, and grinned. 'When it comes to making a friend, you use what the good Lord gave you. And the good Lord gave me a lot.'

'Well, don't lie to me,' I said.

'Don't have to,' she replied. 'You been my buddy since the day you were born. Besides, I don't need to lie around here. The truth is more crazy than anything I could make up.'

That was a fact.

'OK,' Grandma said, and closed the top of the cigar box. 'My jewellery's in order for you. I'm going to die tonight, and that's no lie.'

'No, you aren't!' I said. 'You've been crying wolf for so long that you don't even scare me any more.'

'Well, I don't mean to scare you,' she said. 'I'm just giving you the facts in advance.'

'Grandma, you are fine. You are the picture of health.'

She coughed. 'I am going to die. You got me what I asked for, and now it's time to shove off. As long as you can make friends, you'll be fine in the world.'

'Please don't talk this way,' I begged. 'It really hurts me.'

'Well, think what it does to me,' she shot back with a laugh that became another coughing fit. I patted her on the back until she settled down, then I got her hooked up to her oxygen tank.

'Oh,' she said, over the hissing sound from the hose, 'your mom called. She wants you to come by the salon after school tomorrow. Said she misses you – if you can believe that!'

'I believe it,' I said, feeling a bit hurt. 'I'm missable.'

'Don't get all sensitive on me,' Grandma said. 'I was just fooling. Of course she misses you. Who wouldn't miss the best helper the world has ever known. I think you even beat out Gunga Din.'

'Well, there is nothing wrong with being helpful,' I replied.

'And there is everything wrong with being a doormat,' she said, poking at the air with her cigarette. 'It's a fine line. Think about it.'

That night I tried to think about it because when Grandma said something strongly enough, it usually came true. But I was only thinking in circles. Couldn't I just help someone without thinking they were treating me like a doormat? And even if they thought I was a doormat, wasn't I helping them anyway? Jesus was treated like a doormat but *still* got to do what he wanted.

When I woke up, Grandma was coughing again. I made her tea and got ready for school. 'Are you going to be OK?' I asked, tapping on her curtain.

'Don't worry about me,' she said from the other side. 'I still have a few packs of cigarettes, and I'm so cheap, I won't die till I smoke them all.'

'Take your time,' I said. 'See you later – after I see Mom.'

I left a big bowl of breakfast for Pablo and Pablita and ran out of the house. I passed my little gnome friends. They were part of a Thanksgiving yard scene with Indian corn, and gourds, and a plastic turkey who was being chased by IGOR I HATE YOU because he had the little hatchet. 'Take it easy, Igor,' I said, and bent down and turned him in another direction, then skipped down the street, having done another good deed.

After Mrs Lapp said her 'W.W.J.D.?' I told her Jesus would probably have a special theme park section of heaven set up for Thanksgiving turkeys who lost their heads. After that she got busy on the telephone calling businesses for donations to the community pantry. I read all day, and Olivia listened to a book on tape, which I suspected wasn't a book at all but something else because she was tapping her fingers and humming a tune every now and then. We got along fine except when she lifted off her headphones and wanted to know *exactly* how I was going to sneak her out of the house. I had *exactly* no ideas. 'Still workin' on it,' I said.

'Better put in some overtime,' she replied. 'Because *Godspell* is only playing through the weekend, and if you don't get me there, I'll march down to your grandma and tell her that you are no longer my friend. And that will probably kill her.'

'OK,' I said. 'I'm thinking.' But I wasn't. I knew getting her to *Godspell* was going to be one of those things I figured out at the last minute, like I always did with Mrs Lapp when she asked, 'W.W.J.D.?'

After school I went over to the Beauty and the Beast salon. As soon as Mom saw me she ran over and picked me up and swung me around. 'I've missed you so much,' she said, then stood me up and began fussing with me in a way I just love, as if I'm the only man in the whole world. 'I feel like I don't know you any more.' She kissed me.

'You'll never forget me,' I said, and kissed her back.

'Now sit in my chair,' she said, rubbing her chin as she looked me over. 'I'll trim you up. I want all my men to look good on Thanksgiving.'

'Is Booth coming?' I said.

'Of course he is,' she replied. 'Joey, I know you are a little possessive, but he is a nice guy. He's very good to me and has been especially patient with your dad haunting the town.'

'I'm a nice guy too,' I said. 'How many do you need?'

'I need one nice guy and one Froot Loop.'

'He can be the Loop,' I said.

'OK, Mr Nice Guy, now close your eyes.' She picked up her water bottle and scissors.

I closed them.

'So tell me,' she asked while spraying down my hair and combing it out. 'What's your week been like?'

I didn't tell her much. I didn't tell her I was picked up by the police and finger-printed. I didn't tell her that because it

186

would make us both sad, and we were trying to be happy. I didn't tell her that it was Dad who had stolen Pablo and I had got him back plus Pablita. I didn't tell her that because she hadn't given me permission to keep another dog. I didn't tell her about scaring a blind girl. I didn't tell her that Olivia had become a friend and now I had to sneak her out to see *Godspell*. I didn't tell her that Grandma talked about dying every time she opened her mouth. I didn't tell her I had passed my old school and wanted to return.

So I just told her about the one big thought that filled the space between all the others. 'I miss you all the time,' I said. 'When are you coming home?'

'Believe me,' she replied, snipping away at me, 'I'd love to. But your dad has still been buzzing around, and I don't want him coming over to the house and bugging us there. We have the restraining order, and the police claim it won't be long until they chase him out of town, and then we'll get things back to normal.'

'You promise?' I asked. 'I'd love some *normal* around our house.'

'I promise,' she said. 'Now don't worry.'

Then she swivelled my head this way and that and snipped and snipped until she fluffed it up with some gel and made me look like a little chick that had just pecked its way out of an eggshell.

'I look like Tweety Pie!' I said, staring bug-eyed into the mirror.

'Do you still have that watch Booth gave you?' she asked.

I didn't tell her about that either. And I was lucky that she had an appointment to go over hairstyles with a bride-to-be, so I got a bunch of kisses and squirmed away. I took one last look in the mirror. 'I tawt I taw a puddy tat!' I chirped and ran for the door.

On Wednesday morning I woke up and held my breath all the way from my bed into the living room and didn't breathe again until I saw a cloud of smoke rising from behind the curtain.

'Cup of tea?' I hollered.

'Extra honey,' she called back. 'Soothes my throat.'

'You want biscuits with that?'

'How 'bout some sliced apple?'

'Coming right up,' I hollered back like I

worked in a diner. As I cut up the apple, I called out, 'Grandma, I need some advice about my friend.'

'What's that?' she yelled back.

'I promised Olivia I would sneak her out of her house and take her to see *Godspell* at the opera house because her mother won't let her go, but I don't think I can do it. What would you do?'

'I'd take the bull by the horns,' she said. 'Just look the mother in the eye and ask nicely if she can go. What else can you do? If you try and sneak her out, you only end up looking like Carter sneaking around town. You can't do that. And if the mother says no, then it's Olivia's problem, not yours.'

'But I promised I would sneak her out.'

'Don't make a promise you can't keep,' she said. 'It will catch up with you every time.'

'But I already made the promise,' I said. 'Will you come with us? Maybe Mrs Lapp will let Olivia come if you came along too.'

'I can't go to the opera,' she said. 'Look at me. I'm just barely good enough to sit on the couch all day and lick envelopes. No, you take her. Just ask Mrs Lapp.'

'OK,' I said in a small voice because I

wasn't convinced Grandma's advice would work.

After I fixed her breakfast, I went to the Lapps'. Olivia must have lightened up on her mom because Mrs Lapp was actually being silly with me in a way that she never was. When I knocked on her door, she called out her favourite four letters, and I said, 'He'd always tell the truth.'

She looked disappointed. 'That was too easy,' she said. 'Think of something else.'

'He'd always respect his elders.'

'Keep trying,' she said.

'He'd be nice to the needy.'

'Come on, Joey, put some zip into it.'

'He'd take the day off?'

'You can do better than this,' she said. 'You just don't seem like yourself today. What's wrong?'

I wanted to say Jesus would tell someone's mom that he planned to sneak her daughter out to a show she was forbidden to see, but I didn't. Instead, I squeezed my eyes together and kept thinking.

'Come on,' she coaxed. 'One more time. Make it a good one.'

Then the best answer in the universe just

popped into my head. 'He'd say, Can I get back to you on that!'

'Hmm,' she hummed, and wrote it down.

10.

KNOCK-KNOCK

On Thanksgiving morning, I woke up with a blinding flash going off inside my eyes as if they were filled with exploding stars. I sat up and opened them. Booth was leaning over me with a huge camera and flash attachment mounted on a silver tripod next to my pillow.

He set off the flash again.

'Ouch!' I hollered. And for a few seconds after I opened my eyes I couldn't see anything except for rippling sheets of darkness. I wondered if this was how Olivia felt all the time.

He fired off another flash. 'Stop that!' I hollered, and covered my face with my hands as if he were slapping me around. 'That hurts.'

'I just got a side job with the police taking crime-scene photographs, and I'm practising on you,' he explained. 'Your mom and I have been here for an hour already, and you've been asleep like the dead.'

That reminded me. I threw my covers aside and ran out of my room and across the living room. I ripped open Grandma's curtain. She was sitting in her underwear plucking at her skin and stretching it out into little teepees as if it were made of Silly Putty.

'What do you think you're doing?' she asked.

'Seeing if you are OK,' I replied breathlessly.

'Take a good look,' she said, spreading out her arms. 'I'm alive and damn surprised. I smoked my last cigarette last night, licked my last envelope, and said the "Now I lay me down to sleep" prayer. I fully expected to "die before I wake". That's a fact.'

'Well, you are alive, and it's Thanksgiving so you should be thankful,' I said.

She pointed to her bedside table. There was a green apple with a tooth stuck in it. 'That was one of my last real teeth,' she said. 'I was so sure to be dead, I even tried to eat an apple for my last supper.'

'I'll make sure we have apple sauce,' I said, and held her bony hand. 'Promise.'

She grinned at me. Her gums were caved in like the mouth of a rotten jack-o'-lantern, but I kissed her anyway. *I* was happy she was alive, even if *she* wasn't.

'Now run up to that grocery store and get me some smokes,' she squawked. 'Now that I'm still alive, I need to keep killing myself.' She reached into her pillowcase and pulled out a scratch card. 'Here,' she said, 'this one is a ten-dollar winner. Buy yourself a treat while you're at it.'

'Yes,' I said. 'Yeah.' And I was so glad she was her grumpy old self, I nearly flew out of the house except I saw Mom in the kitchen surrounded by bags of food.

'Mom!' I shouted.

'Joey!' she hollered back. She dropped down onto one knee, and I ran right at her and hit her like a cannonball. She fell back and would have hit the floor except she hit the cabinets so hard I heard a few things fall over inside.

'Oh, my,' she winced, and rolled her shoulders around. 'Have you got stronger since I last squeezed you?'

'Yes!' I shouted, and made a muscle.

She felt it. 'Well, Mr Helpful,' she said, reading the label I had stuck to my forehead before bed, 'I'm going to need some muscle today. We have a turkey as big as the Macy's parade balloon, and not only am I going to need some help with it, but you are going to have to eat a ton.'

'I can do that,' I said, and chattered my teeth together like those wind-up jaws. 'I can do whatever you want. You name it, and I'll do it.' I put my arms around her and licked her face.

'Stop that,' she said. 'You're worse than Pablo.'

'I've missed you,' I whimpered. 'So much that I had to get another dog.'

'I noticed,' she said. 'And I think we need to talk about that.'

'OK,' I said, 'I love to talk.' But before we could get started, she suddenly jumped up and marched towards the front door. She opened it and cocked her ear to one side and listened.

'What are you listening for?' I asked.

'Hush,' she said, and raised her hand for silence.

I stopped in my tracks and listened alongside her. In the air was the roar of a motorcycle. It didn't sound like it was moving anywhere but just pent up with the engine revving like a rodeo bull held back by a gate and waiting, waiting to spring forward. I knew Dad was out there somewhere. He was getting ready to cut loose, and she knew it too.

But when she turned away and lowered her hand, she was beaming down at me as if there was nothing to worry about, so I said, 'I have to go to the store. Do you need anything?'

'Why don't you stay home with me?' she said in her parent voice that made a question sound like a direct order. 'I need you to sharpen all the knives and help me cook. Booth can go get Grandma's smokes.'

'OK,' I said, and leaned my face into her. I sniffed her clothes. I sniffed her arms. I jumped up and down and sniffed her hair until she grabbed the top of my head with one hand and pressed me down like she was loading one of those springy joke snakes into a can. Then in one quick move she ripped the MR HELPFUL label off my forehead. 'Owww!' I hollered. 'You got some skin with that.'

'Is that all?' she asked, turning the label over and examining the sticky side. 'I thought I pulled out some of your nuttiness.'

I hugged her. I was so happy to have her back home. I didn't think of anything bad, and all I could think was that Thanksgiving was the holiday with the best name, and I wondered if I put a TURKEY label on my forehead Mom would just stuff me full of love and hugs and kisses and everything good in the world to be thankful for.

'Booth,' she called over my head. He came sprinting out of my room as if Mom were on fire. She really had him trained.

'Yes, Fran?' he asked, all breathless, his eyes darting around looking for danger. It seemed like he expected to find something wrong, like when Dad had peeked in the window and Mom threw a glass at him. I knew they had been living in a motel and hiding from Dad, and I thought there might be some things they weren't telling me. It made me feel all nervous inside because I figured if she was hiding something from me, something awful, then I wouldn't be able to help her solve it.

'Go get Grandma some smokes,' she said to Booth.

I handed him the scratch card and gave him Grandma's instructions. 'And with the extra money, please get me some turkey jerky for the dogs.'

'Will do,' he said, being his jolly self, then headed out the door.

And take your time, I thought, but didn't say it.

Mom opened a kitchen drawer and clawed around inside it until she pulled out three long knives. One had a big V missing right in the middle of the blade and a bunch of little nicks around it from where I had used the knife to hack open a lock on what I thought was a pirate's chest down in the basement but when I finally got the lock off there was only a stack of dresses that Grandma later told me were hers from when she was a farm girl and used to sew up a storm. Some of the dresses had blue ribbons pinned to them from winning prizes for dressmaking at the county fair. Grandma had washed a few of them out and ironed them, and they were hanging in the hall closet. I wanted her to try one on, but she insisted they were only for special old lady occasions, or a yard sale.

'Can you sharpen these?' Mom asked, and gave me a round sharpener that you put the blade of the knife into and roll back and forth on the counter.

'Yeah,' I said. 'That's easy.'

And the rest of the morning was just as easy as rolling that sharpening wheel back and forth across the counter. Mom got the turkey cleaned up and stuffed with those little bags of crunchy stuffing and popped it into the oven. Then we peeled a sack of apples and cored them and made farm-style apple sauce with cinnamon and lots of brown sugar poured in. Later she had me open all the cans for the side dishes – cranberry sauce, creamed corn, tiny peas, and sauerkraut because it was Grandma's favourite. I knew where every can came from in the grocery store. I could tell you the aisle and section and whether it was on the top, middle, or bottom shelf. I could give you the price per item. And as I opened the cans, I thought this was exactly my idea of Thanksgiving. I was so thankful everything was in order. No surprises. No secrets. Nothing sneaking up on me and making me nervous. Just everything right there on the counter where I could see it.

She also had a tube of crescent rolls from the cold case of the grocery store, and a box of potatoes you just add hot water to, in case the real potatoes she bought were no good because they had so many eyes in them. Booth had brought several bottles of bubbly wine called Cold Duck, and she drank some out of a tall iced-tea glass, and Grandma had a mug of it while she sat on the couch and watched the Green Bay Packers beat up on the Detroit Lions. I just couldn't stay away from Mom, and I did everything she asked me to do, and it wasn't until she began to boil a big pot of water and cut the eyes out of the potatoes that I remembered about the Lapps bringing dessert.

'Wonderful,' Mom said. 'I spoke to Mrs Lapp yesterday. I called to see how you were doing, and she said you and Olivia were working well together.'

'Yeah,' I said. 'But she's become a lot nicer since she came to the house to meet Grandma.'

Over the roar of the TV crowd Grandma shouted, 'I taught her some manners.'

'Well,' Mom said to me, 'you should be very proud of yourself.'

'I am,' I said smiling brightly. 'I think Mrs Lapp should give me an A for Helpfulness. Olivia wasn't easy, but I wore her down.'

'That's one of your best qualities,' Mom remarked. 'You could wear a mountain down into a molehill.'

'That boy's an unrelenting force!' Grandma shouted. 'I bet they name a hurricane after him someday, and he blows us all to kingdom come.'

I looked up at Mom and rolled my eyes. 'She's always talking about dying,' I whispered.

'That's a subject she should get an A in,' Mom whispered back.

'What's your best subject?' I asked.

'Putting up with you,' she said, and gave me a smack on the bottom. 'Now get busy setting the table, and I'll finish off these potatoes.'

'Should I use the good tablecloth?'

'Yes,' she said. 'No plastic today.'

I got the old lace tablecloth out of the linen closet. I spread it out on the table and put the pink stain where a glass of red wine had spilled down on Booth's end. I had made some Thanksgiving crafts at the Lapps' and decorated the centre with drawings of pilgrims and Indians and a Styrofoam turkey I painted brown and red with real turkey feathers fanned out and stuck in the tail with little turkey-feet we made out of twigs. Once I had the plates and cutlery and glasses and napkins set out, I ran to my room and got my label gun. I made a place name for each of us. I put POCAHONTAS on Mom's plate, SITTING BULL on Booth's, SQUANTO on Grandma's even though Squanto was a man, and mine was the best – GERONIMO! – because it was one of my favourite names in the world. Then I set two plates in a corner of the kitchen floor and labelled one LITTLE BEAR and the other LITTLE TREE for our little dogs.

Finally, the turkey was cooked, the

potatoes were whipped, and the side dishes were in serving bowls. I attached a long extension cord to the electric carving knife, and we were ready. Mom made me change into a nice white shirt and good pants, but I looked silly because the cuffs on the shirt were halfway to my elbows and I couldn't even button them, and the cuffs on my pants were a couple inches above my ankles. Booth fixed up his big camera on the tripod and set the self-timer, and we all stood to one side of the table and smiled until he made us do it three times in a row and by then we were so hungry we were all chewing on our lips.

We took our places, and even before I could say the blessing, the doorbell rang. I thought it was the Lapps. Mom hopped up. 'I wonder what this is?' she said to no one in particular as she strolled over to the door. 'Maybe a neighbour needs to borrow some flour.' But when she opened the door she was surprised. Nobody was there. Instead there was a huge basketful of roses. Yellow roses. I knew they were Mom's favourite, and I looked over at Booth to see if he had a sneaky look on his face as if he had sent them.

But he looked puzzled, and I turned back to look at Mom. Her face tightened, and she stepped around the roses and onto the porch. She looked up the street, then down the street. She stood with her head cocked to one side like a dog listening for something.

Then she shrugged, turned, and picked up the basket by its braided handle. A little card fell out of the roses. Before she stepped back into the house, she picked it up and flicked it open with her nail. Her face hardened, and she slipped it into her shirt pocket.

'Look at these wonderful flowers,' she said pleasantly. She set them down next to the table.

'Who sent them?' Booth asked.

'The girls at work,' she said.

Grandma kicked me under the table, and I knew what she knew: girls didn't say hello with roses.

'Very thoughtful,' Booth remarked, standing up. He reached forward and leaned over the table so he could pour Cold Duck in everyone's glass except mine. I had chocolate milk. When he sat down, he raised his glass and said, 'I'd like to make a toast.'

But before he could get all his words out, the doorbell rang.

'I'll get it!' Mom said, and she dashed over to the door and pulled it open.

From where I was sitting, I could see there were three pie boxes stacked up on the porch. She stepped over them and clomped down the stairs in her high heels. She looked up the street and down. Then she turned, climbed the stairs, picked up the pies, and brought them inside.

'Well,' she said cheerfully, 'seems like we have another gift from the girls.' She took them to the kitchen, then returned to her seat.

'A toast,' Booth began again, 'to family and friends,' he said quickly. 'You can't choose your family, but you sure can choose your friends, and I can't think of a better place for me to be today than among you all.'

Just then the doorbell rang again and Mom was up and out of her seat like a spooked cat. She whipped open the door. There was a six-pack of canned beer. She picked it up and heaved it off the porch. It hit the sidewalk and skidded into the road. Then she stepped back inside and turned the dead bolt on the door.

'What was that?' Booth asked.

'Nothing,' Mom said decisively, as if that word were a dead bolt to the truth. 'Let's eat.' She handed me the electric carving knife and a serving fork, and I could see her hands shaking a bit. 'Joey, you carve the turkey,' she said.

I had always wanted to carve a turkey. I thought I'd carve it up like one of those silly grinning monkeys coconut sculptures people brought back from vacationing in Florida. I clicked the switch on just as the doorbell rang.

Mom was out of her seat in a flash.

'Here we go,' Grandma said just when Mom unlocked the door and yanked it open. 'She's sinkin' to his level again.'

Nobody was there. On the threshold was a little box like the kind you get at the jewellery store when you buy a ring. Mom stepped over it and stood on the porch wish her hands on her hips. She looked as sturdy as a lighthouse with her eyes searching back and forth. Then she must have got an idea.

She ran back inside, grabbed the electric knife out of my hand, and returned to the porch with the extension cord slithering behind her.

'See this!' Mom said. Without opening the little box, she began to saw it in half. It took her a minute to cut through, and once she did, she set down the knife and flipped open one of the lids. Half a ring fell out and bounced on the porch. Mom picked it up and examined it, then raised it above her head. 'Cheap creep!' she hollered to no one we could see. 'It's plastic!'

In a minute I could hear Dad's motorcycle. Even with the engine idling, it still sounded like something angry spitting fire. Mom came back inside and got the basket of roses. By then Dad had pulled up in front of the house and turned off the engine.

'Hi, Fran,' he said, and removed his bug-eyed sunglasses.

'See these,' she snarled, pointing to the flowers. 'This is what I would like to do to you.' Then she began to cut all the blossoms off the roses.

'Fran,' Booth said as he got up and walked towards the door. 'I know you're upset, but maybe it's time for us to settle down and be thankful for what we have and just let him go on his way.'

She turned off the knife and stepped back inside. 'You're right,' she said. 'I'm not going to let that creep ruin our dinner.'

She returned to her place at the table and took a deep breath and shivered wildly as if she were Houdini trying to escape from inside her own skin.

Then we could hear him walk up the steps.

'I'll call the cops,' Booth said evenly. He headed for the phone.

Grandma lit a cigarette and exhaled. She had a smile on her face like a satisfied snake. She must have seen this coming.

There was a knock at the door. 'Fran,' Dad said, 'I'm trying to be nice. Don't you remember how nice I used to be to you?'

From her chair Mom threw the salt shaker and hit the glass pane on the door. It shattered and in an instant revealed Dad on the other side. He had his hands over his face to shield his eyes, and he stepped back and began to pluck at his leather clothes to shake the shards of glass off.

'Good Lord, Fran,' he said. 'Is that any way to greet a family member on Thanksgiving?'

'You don't deserve a family!' she yelled. 'Now get out of here and stop ruining this one.'

'Let me talk to Joey,' he said.

'No!' she hollered from her chair.

'I want to see my mom,' he said. 'Wish her a happy Thanksgiving.'

'I have a restraining order out against you,' she said fiercely. 'You have to stay a hundred yards away.'

Dad shrugged. 'Restraining orders are for criminals,' he said. 'I'm a *lover*!' He puckered his lips way out. 'Kiss me,' he said. 'Your kiss will fix me up and patch us back together. I know I've been a clown, but now I'm ready to be a good husband. Kiss me.'

'I'll give you one in the kisser,' Mom said.

'Fran,' Booth called out from the kitchen, 'just stay put. The police are on their way.'

Mom was out of her seat before he finished his sentence. She rushed to the door with a long knife in her hand, and Dad backed up.

Booth ran into the living room and snatched his video camera out of the case. He raised it to his eye and began filming as he slowly moved towards the door.

Mom chased Dad off the porch, and he scrambled down the stairs. He stood there in front of the house calling for me. 'Joey, son,' he pleaded as if trying to coax a cat out of a tree. 'Come and say Happy Thanksgiving to me.'

I wanted to. I was his son, and there was something powerful in me that wanted to help him. I was pushing my chair back from the table when Grandma grabbed my wrist.

'Don't you dare,' she growled like a watchdog. 'It's bad enough to witness this mess, but don't get caught up in it. I told you, they're nuts. Just look at me. I'm worn out from living like this.'

Just then Mom hollered. 'I told you the next time you came around here, I was going to throw a knife right between your eyes.' And she reared back and let it fly.

It would have hit the man in the moon between the eyes before it hit Dad. The knife spun end over end and clattered onto the sidewalk across the street.

'Missed me, missed me, now you have to kiss me,' Dad sang.

Mom stormed back into the house. She grabbed the pies from their boxes and returned to the porch and threw them at him one at a time. The strange thing is he never moved, and she never hit him. He never ducked out of the way. He just stood there with his face leaning way forward, daring her, when the first pie hit the sidewalk and skidded into the gutter. Then the next pie hit the yard with a thump. The third pie slipped out of Mom's hand, caught the upper edge of the porch ceiling, and fell straight down and burst open, splattering her shoes with pumpkin mush. She grabbed the flower basket by the handle and flung it at him. It missed, and the glass vase inside pitched forward and broke against the concrete. She marched back inside and scanned the counter, searching for the other knives. But by then Booth had put down his camera and tossed them out the back door. It was a good thing because Mom looked ready to run down the steps and stab him. Instead, she grabbed the bottle of Cold Duck by the neck, marched outside, and flung it with all her might. It wobbled through the air and exploded against the fender of a parked car, like when a bottle is smashed on the side of a newly launched ship.

Dad just stood there as if he could catch bullets in his teeth. 'Joey,' he called out, 'you said all I had to do is be nice to her and she'd be nice back. What gives?'

'Did you tell him to do this?' Mom yelled at me from the doorway with such fury that I froze. 'Did you tell him to try and win me back? After all I've done for you. I can't believe you'd turn on me and team up with him. *That* is a stab in the back!'

'Don't blame the boy,' Dad said.

'You shut up!' Mom shouted. 'I want to hear what Joey has to say for himself.'

She put her hands on her hips and gritted her teeth as she stared over at me. 'Well?' she asked. 'What do you have to say for yourself?'

I wasn't sure what to say. I had said something like that to him when I went to find the Chihuahuas. But I was only trying to help. I wanted him to be a good dad. But now I just wanted him to go away.

I lowered my head and shrugged.

'How could you?' Mom snapped at me. 'What are you two up to?' Her head whipped back and forth between me and Dad. But neither of us had an answer.

And then I saw Mrs Lapp and Olivia standing on the sidewalk by the edge of our front yard. I didn't know how long they had been standing there, but even if it was just a little bit, it was still too much. I hadn't seen them coming because I was watching Mom and Dad so intently. Mrs Lapp looked absolutely pale with fear, and the bright green Key lime pie she was carrying in her white-gloved hands was shaking like a bowl of terrified Jell-O. Olivia's face was turned up towards her, and I could read her lips saying, 'What? What's going on?' She tried to step forward, but her mom turned her around, and they marched down the side-walk back towards their home.

'Olivia!' I shouted. 'Come back!' Just when I made a friend, my family put on a freak show and scared my friend away. The only thing I could think to myself was, What would Joey do? I bolted out of my chair before Grandma could grab me, and I took off running out the back door, past the knives, across the yard, and into the cemetery and around, and I got to the Lapps' house first and was standing in front of the door when Mrs Lapp and Olivia arrived.

'Please move out of the way,' Mrs Lapp said.

'I have something to say,' I replied, a little out of breath.

No, I have something to say,' she said sternly. 'I don't think you should come back here any more. I've been thinking a lot about you just now. I asked, What would Jesus do? and he told me. Keep Joey away from your daughter. So please don't come back any more. We try very had to provide a good loving home for Olivia, and I know she has some issues we need to work on. *I'm* not blind. But what I saw at your house was just too much. You and your family have a lot of problems that we just don't want to share. I'm sorry,' she said, 'but I have to draw the line somewhere when it comes to protecting Olivia.'

'But what happened?' Olivia asked, still holding her pie as if she were about to set it on a shelf. 'Someone please tell me.'

I looked at Mrs Lapp. She shook her head back and forth, and I knew not to say anything to Olivia so I did as she asked and stepped away from the door.

'Joey, it's just time to admit that we'd all be better off going our own separate ways. You either have God in your daily life or you have chaos,' she said. 'I made my choice a long time ago, and I'm sticking with it.'

'I'm just trying to help everyone be better,' I explained.

'That's God's job,' she said.

'Can't I help too? My grandma said God helps those who help themselves.'

'Mom!' Olivia shouted. 'What is going on!'

''Bye, Joey,' Mrs Lapp said. And just like that she shifted her pie to one hand, opened the door with her other, and directed Olivia across the threshold. Then she followed and closed the door. Even still I could hear Olivia shouting. 'What happened? What bad thing happened? Don't treat me like a baby. Tell me, or I'll throw this pie!'

I had heard enough. On the way home

from the Lapps' house, I mostly looked down at my feet. When I passed the yard where my gnome friends lived, I looked over to see if they had made it through the holiday. Someone had knocked them over and left them face down in the dirt as if they had given them the boot and banished them from under the bushes. Then I looked up. There was a cop car stopped in front of my house. I could hear the radio squawking. 'Carter Pigza! Carter Pigza! Suspect last seen on Plum Street heading north.'

I lowered my head and ran for the house. As I climbed the steps, I saw the cranberry sauce and sauerkraut and creamed corn and bowls and serving spoons on the sidewalk. The turkey was on the porch looking as if it had come to life and had tried to make a break for it. I kicked it out of the way.

'Where's Mom?' I shouted when I passed through the door. There was still the glass and food mess and chopped-up flowers, and Grandma sitting at the table smoking another cigarette with her eyes closed. Her elbow was in the centre of her empty dinner plate with her chin tucked into her fist. When she lifted her eyelids, her eyes peeked out like a crocodile's. She raised her chin and slowly opened her hand one finger at a time. I read her mind. This was bad thing number five. 'Where's Mom?' I asked again. She flicked her ashes towards the bathroom.

I knocked on the door. 'Mom?'

'Come in,' she said.

I did. She had just stepped out of the shower. Her hair was wet and sticking to her neck, and she had a bath towel wrapped around her middle. The light was off.

'What else happened?' I asked. 'I heard the police.'

'Nothing,' she said.

I knew she was not telling me the truth. I asked her again what had happened because I don't like it when she keeps something from me. She's not allowed. Because when she lies, something inside me changes, and its like the *whole world* is one way and I'm the other. Like I can't trust a thing, as if the whole world knows a secret I don't and I'm running around from person to person asking them to tell me but they won't and the more I don't know what is going on the more scared I become and I feel myself drifting farther and farther away from everyone.

'So where are you and Booth staying?' I asked.

'Around,' she said, brushing out her hair.

'Where around?' I asked.

'Just around,' she said, treating me as if I were Dad's little spy. 'Your grandma knows.'

And I was so upset when she said that, I just squeezed my eyes tightly until I could see stars, as if Booth were setting off his flash again.

'Where's Booth?' I asked.

'I'm not sure,' she said.

'Well, what are we going to do?'

'About what?' she asked.

'About *everything*,' I said, nearly melting down to nothing. 'Our house, Dad, us – you know, what just happened. How do we fix all this?'

'This is my problem, not yours, so don't worry about it,' she said as if she was so tired she didn't care one way or another. 'Now, can I have a little privacy?'

I stepped out of the bathroom and closed the door behind me. I could hear her lock it. I felt so full of sadness on a day when I was supposed to feel so full of thanks. It was as if all the stuffing had been knocked out of me. Then I had one more ugly feeling, a feeling I didn't understand – a feeling that didn't come with a label attached to it. It was such an awful feeling it made me hate myself, even though I knew I should hate her. But since I couldn't hate her, I lowered my head and walked away.

11

smithereens

In the morning, I looked in my mirror and ripped the WHAT, ME WORRY? label off my forehead because I was worried. I was getting ready to go to Olivia's, and even though Mrs Lapp had expelled me from her house as if she were the principal of a two-kid school, I wanted to get back to her on something. I wanted to ring her doorbell as if it were a fire alarm and ask, What happens when your secret helper needs help? Because I needed some. And even though I was changing my patches every day, and taking deep breaths, watching my 'p's and 'q's, walking a tight line, following the rules, and helping out, I was beginning to feel very springy inside. I was beginning to believe that all my help was worth nothing, and that made me feel like nothing too. A big zero. That's what I woke up with inside my chest. A big, quivering, nervous zero, and it was making me very uncomfortable because that zero was getting bigger and bigger and it was filling up my insides like an inner tube so that I felt like if that zero got any bigger it would blow me to smithereens, just like our family was blown to smithereens and our house was blown to smithereens and my hope to help everyone was being blown to smithereens.

I couldn't stand lying in bed and thinking about my family any more so I got up and went into the kitchen. While the water boiled, I cut up apples into little matchstick-sized strips. Grandma liked apples because they kept her regular, and I liked cutting them up because it gave me something to do.

After I poured the water into the teapot, I could hear the hissing noise of her oxygen hose. Sometimes the breathing tube slipped off her nose when she slept, or she just removed it and set it aside while she smoked another cigarette.

I set the breakfast tray on a TV table outside her curtain like I had done for weeks. 'Grandma,' I called out, 'time to get up.'

I just heard the hissing.

'Grand-maaaa!' I hollered.

Nothing.

I closed my eyes and reached for the edge of the curtain. My hand was suddenly shaking and so was my voice. 'Ladies and gentlemen,' I announced to Pablo and Pablita, who had come out looking for food, 'I give you the one, the only, Grandma Pigza! The woman whose brain has been surgically replaced with a crystal ball!' I whipped the shower curtain back and gasped when I opened my eyes. She was sitting there on the couch all dressed up in one of her old blue-ribbon dresses that was made from a print of summer flowers. But her body was in a different season. She looked like a dried-up sunflower inside that dress with her thin neck bent forward and her chin dug into her chest. Even her drooping shoulders looked like fall leaves that had lost their colour. 'Grandma!' I whispered nervously. 'Wake up.' I bent over to one side to I could look up into her face. It was so still. I turned her oxygen tank off. Then I reached for her hand. It felt odd, not cold, just heavy. 'Grandma?' I whispered again. 'Grandma?'

She didn't answer and I already knew why. 'Look,' I said, 'wake up. I'm taking my patch off my arm.' I ripped it off. 'And I'm putting it on your arm. It's a fresh one and that should wind your clock.'

That didn't work and I was getting scared like when you know something has gone bad and you can't do anything to stop it. So I ran back into my room and slapped two patches onto my arm because it was definitely going to be a two-patch day.

Then I got a little mirror from the bathroom and held it under her nose. She didn't fog it up. I put that down and tried to check her pulse, but I couldn't feel anything. I got a flashlight and lifted a soft eyelid, which was slumped down against the bottom of her eye like a flat tyre.

'Grandma,' I whispered, 'if you are a zombie, what is the cure to bring you back to life?'

But she didn't stomp or scratch or wiggle.

She didn't get back to me. Finally I lit one of her cigarettes and took a puff and blew the smoke in her face, and she didn't perk up or snatch the cigarette out of my hand or back-slap me for smoking. Then I knew she was dead.

Her clock had stopped and even though I didn't want my clock to stop, I did want to slow time for a while. I wanted us to be alone before anyone came over and ruined the quiet time we had left together. The first thing I did was lay her back down on the couch because I knew she was going to get stiff soon like bodies do in the movies and I didn't want her to fall off the couch and hit the floor and look as if I didn't care. 'You can rest now,' I said as I straightened out her thin legs and pulled up her socks so that they were the same height on both sides, and I adjusted her slippers so her bony feet looked comfortable. I knew enough to fold her hands across her lap. Then I tugged on the hem of her dress to smooth out the wrinkles and once I did that I sat there and stared down at her. It's true what they say that when someone you love dies, you only remember the good things about them.

Whatever hurtful things she had ever said or done all vanished, and I felt as if I had lost the one person who understood me better than anyone else. We *were* alike. And that's why she wanted me to move on in the world, so I wouldn't end up dying on a couch behind a shower curtain in someone else's house.

I took a good look at her. She was grey, and the dress she wore was so old, as if she too were something slowly fading away. I went into Mom's room and get her bright red nail polish and some lipstick and make-up. When I returned, I pulled up a chair and began to fix her up the same way I had watched Mom fix her up when they would have a little day of beauty.

I rubbed lipstick on my finger, then ran it over her lips until her smile took on some shape. Then I dusted her cheeks and nose with powder so she whitened up a bit, but not so much that she looked like a marble statue. I brushed her short hair forward as best I could and with my fingers evened out her bangs. The longer hairs on the side of her head I tucked behind her ears. I leaned down and examined her earlobes. They were pierced but empty. I went into Mom's room and found a pair of small silver studs. When I returned to Grandma, I pushed the studs through the holes. I couldn't find the backs to hold them in place, but it didn't matter. She wasn't going anywhere.

When I began to paint her fingernails, I started remembering so much about her. Maybe it was because I was holding her hand again after having spent so much of my life with her hand grabbing onto me. Even though we were both wired when it was just the two of us in the old days. I had more energy than she did, and when she wanted to take a nap or at night when she was tired, she sometimes would tie our hands together with one of Dad's neckties, or a scarf, or old belt so I couldn't run off. Sometimes I'd keep scissors in my pocket so I could cut myself free and sneak away, until I made too much noise, and then she'd tie us up again. I remember her hands holding cards from one time when our heat was turned off from not paying the bill, and we went across to the Mini Mart and hung out for the night. Grandma made a fake campfire out of those paper logs they sell, and we sat cross-legged on either side and drank strawberry Yoo-Hoos and ate marshmallows we stuck on drink straws and pretended were roasted while we played a thousand games of crazy eights until it was light outside and we could go shopping in heated stores until we ended up in some downtown office waiting for ever until she got our heat turned back on. And when I held her ring finger, I remembered when we went to a jeweller and she sold her little diamond wedding band so we could get some cash because she was trying to keep things going while Mom and Dad were so busy chasing around they forgot about us. I just wished her hands would come back to life and grip me again like they used to. I wouldn't care if she grabbed me by the back of my shirt and swung me around until I was so dizzy I fell down and curled up into a ball and gave her five minutes of peace. Or if she poked me or squeezed me or slapped at me or jerked my arm so hard I thought I'd lose it, like when you jerk a baseball bat out of a rack. Now, her hands were no longer around to tell me what to do, and it was my hands that had to hold hers.

When I finished her nails I held her wrists and waved them back and forth so they would dry. And then I remembered something I had done that made me feel so bad all over again. When I had left Dad's house in Pittsburgh last summer, the last thing I saw was Grandma standing on his porch waving at me, and even though at first I thought she was waving goodbye, she told me when she came back to our house by bus a few weeks later that she was waving so we would turn around and rescue her too. I always felt bad about that, especially when she said she thought I loved Pablo more than I loved her. I told her it had nothing to do with love, that we were just too scared Dad was going to get us, and so we left in a hurry. But although her feelings were hurt, she came back to help me even though I didn't know I still needed her help. She knew Mom and Dad were not finished with each other, and it was up to her to get me out of this crazy house so I could have a chance to be somebody besides Carter and Fran's wired-up kid.

'I'm so glad you came back, Grandma,' I whispered. By the time I finished saying that, I was unable to see with all the tears in my eyes. I leaned forward and wiped them on her bony shoulder, and I kept my face pressed there because I knew my final time with her was over.

When I sat up, I tried to take care of the business she left behind. I looked in her cigar box to see if there was any jewellery I could put on her. There were a few hairpins and a Girl Scout badge for gardening and some plastic kid's rings and clip-on flowers. There was also an address book. I opened it up. Listed inside were a few scratched-out names and nothing more. She had no friends. None. And now I knew why she wanted me to make friends. She wanted me to have what she couldn't.

She had stuck an envelope between the cushions of the couch as if she had raised a white flag and given up. The envelope had been marked *'Lung Transplant'*. She had crossed that out and written *'For Joey P. Pigza'*. The P stands for Petunia. That was her pet name for me when I was a baby, and so she always used P for my middle initial. For some reason Mom didn't give me a middle name. She was going to name me after Carter but they were having an argument about what to call me, and so she just gave me the first name. Once Grandma decided I didn't always smell like a petunia, she called me Piglet. Then I grew some and she called me Popeye. For a while she called me the Pope, Popsicle, Pit Stop, Putz, Pizza, Purple, and Pluto, and when I was driving her nuts, she called me Joey *Problem* Pigza. Once she said it stood for Paul – my twin brother. She said, 'You had both been put up for adoption, and he had been taken in by a nice family, but no one would take you so we had to keep you. Somewhere out there in a really nice house, with nice parents and an especially nice grandma, lives a little boy named Paul J. Pigza, who is treated like a prince. If you ever meet him, ask what the J stands for.' I called all three Pigzas in the phone book and there wasn't one with a middle name of Joey. After about a week Grandma told me she was just pulling my leg. I think she would have allowed me to go on believing that I had a twin brother except that she wanted to see my reaction when she told me I didn't. That was her idea of a good joke. It took me a while to laugh, but I did eventually because I realized that if I did have a great twin, Grandma would have kept him, and that would have to be me. So I was the great one after all.

I opened the envelope. There was three hundred dollars in cash, six scratch card winners that added up to fifty bucks, and two pieces of folded paper. On one she had written on the outside MY LAST WILL AND TESTAMENT. I flipped it open. *Everything goes to Joey*, she had written. *Nothing goes to them.* It was signed and dated one week ago. She knew she was going to go. She was just waiting for me to make a friend. I opened the other. *Joey*, it read, *after you read this call Galt's Funeral Parlour. They'll take care of me. I already talked with them and paid in advance. I'll be cremated, and put in a jar for you and Pablo.* And then she had added just in the last few days, *and Pablita. Love, Grandma. PS: Look out for number seven.* She must have known her death was bad thing number six. Now I had to look out for one more. What could be worse than this?

Just then there was a knock on what was

left of our front door and I nearly jumped to the ceiling. Pablo and Pablita began barking furiously.

When I opened the door, I saw it was the little old lady with the ice cream.

'Sorry I'm a few days late,' she said sweetly.

'Believe me,' I replied, 'it's better this way.'

'Did you know there is a turkey on your front porch?' she asked. 'I think some rodents got to it.'

'Oh thanks,' I said. She held out a plastic container of ice cream. 'For the dogs,' she said. 'Charro wanted me to say thank you again.'

I took it. 'I'd invite you in,' I said. 'But my grandma is having a bad day, and the house is a bit of a mess, and nobody is here but me and Pablo and Pablita, and so it's just not a good time.'

'Oh,' she replied. 'Do you need some help?'

'No,' I said. 'It's OK. My grandma left instructions what to do.

Talking to her seemed to settle me down a bit, and after she left, I got started cleaning up. I took a big trash bag out front and slid the gnawed-on turkey inside. I imagined the little gnomes from down the street had discovered it and spent the evening on my porch chopping at the turkey meat with their little hatchets and slurping up the stuff on the steps. They were probably stuffed and sleeping it off under some bushes. I walked down the steps and threw everything I could in the bag – bowls, spoons, forks, plates, pie tins. Everything. Then I dragged the bag out back to the trash can. I pulled the hose around front and sprayed off the steps and a little bit of the porch where I could without getting water inside the house because of the busted door. When I finished that, I returned inside and called the funeral parlour.

'She's on the couch. The door's open. You can just come and get her,' I said to the man who said he had spoken to her. 'And there's some home-made ice cream in the freezer. Help yourself.'

'Will you be there?' he asked. 'There are some papers to sign.'

'No,' I said. 'I have to go tell my mom. And I'll tell her to stop by and sign.'

'OK,' he said. 'Don't worry. We'll take care of her from here, and we'll set the viewing for Sunday.'

'Thanks,' I said, then thought to add, 'Be gentle with her. She's had a pretty rough life.'

'We'll treat her like royalty,' he said. 'She'll be in good hands.'

When I got off the phone I went over to Grandma. I peeled a second patch off and stuck it on her shoulder, up under her sleeve, next to the other one. 'This is so you don't get too nervous at the pearly gates and give Saint Peter an earful,' I said. 'Remember, if you don't have anything good to say, don't say anything at all.'

Then I locked the dogs in my bedroom with the turkey jerky and went to tell Mom.

When I walked into the hair salon she was doing six girls at once. I stood and watched for a minute. There was a wedding about to take place, and Mom was brushing out hair and pinning up hair and spraying hair, and all the girls were putting on purple satin gowns and squeezing their feet into shoes that were tight and tall, and Booth was there snapping rolls of pictures, and when I realized they would never slow down I just inched right up to Mom and said, 'I have something big to tell you.'

'Well, it better be an apology,' she said, sounding just as irritated as when I last saw her. Then she combed her fingers through some girl's hair and teased it back and forth until the girl's neck about snapped off.

'It's not about Dad,' I said.

'I'm still very annoyed that you spoke to him about me.'

'I was trying to help him feel a little better,' I said.

'Well, that's no help to me.'

'Or me,' I said. 'I'm the one who's stuck in the middle.'

'Well, you are going to have to choose – me or him,' she said, turning towards me. 'so what is your choice?'

'Can I get back—'

Mom reached forward and covered my mouth with her open hand. 'I hate it when you say that!' she snapped. 'It really sends me around the bend.'

I bit down on the inside of her palm, and she jerked it away. 'OK,' I said, 'I won't say it.'

'You're driving me crazy,' she huffed, rubbing her hands together.

'Mom,' I said. 'I came here to tell you that Grandma died.'

Everyone seemed to stop as if we were playing freeze tag.

'I had a feeling something like this would happen,' Mom said, lowering her brush and sighing. She seemed more frustrated than sad. 'The minute I try to get ahead, something always goes wrong.' She began to pull little brown clouds of hair out of the brush and drop them on the floor.

'Don't worry. I already called the funeral parlour,' I said, not wanting to ruin her day. 'The viewing is Sunday. You have to go over there and sign some papers. I've taken care of everything else, and now I'm going to go find Dad.'

'Fran,' Booth said, lowering his camera, 'why don't you go with Joey?'

She began to brush another girl's hair. 'I'm pretty busy here,' she said. 'I'll see him tonight. Besides, there's nothing I can do now anyway.'

'Go on,' Booth said calmly. 'We're about set anyway. The girls look fine.'

'I still have the bride to style,' Mom said. 'Joey can deal with his dad. There's no telling what I'd do to the man if I saw him.'

'Then just spend some time with Joey,' he coaxed. 'Come on.'

'Booth,' Mum said harshly, 'this is one of those times when you are not family and should mind your own business.'

Booth dropped his gaze down into the viewfinder of his camera and took a shot of his own feet.

'I was just trying to help,' I said. 'Is that so wrong?'

'I'll tell you what would be a help to me – don't ever mention that man's name around me again. That would be a *real* help.'

'Would that make you happy?' I asked.

'It wouldn't hurt my chances of ever smiling again,' she replied.

Suddenly Booth raised his camera to his eye. 'Smile,' he called to Mom. She glared over at him, and he snapped her picture. I knew she had dots in her eyes from the flash, so I just darted out the front door. By the time she could see, she'd find I was out of sight, and I figured that would make her happy.

It only took me a few minutes to make my

way up to the stockyards. And a few more to find Dad's little shack. I peeked in the window again. This time he wasn't surrounded by yapping Chihuahuas. I tapped on the wood over the window. When he rolled over, I could hear the sound of bottles clinking against each other.

'Dad,' I called out. 'It's me, Joey.'

He stood up, and I went around to meet him at the front door.

'What's up?' he asked, yawning and rubbing his eyes.

'Grandma died today,' I said.

He looked down at the ground and slowly rubbed the dirt with the sole of his shoe as if she were buried under his feet.

'I hate it when someone older than me dies,' he said. 'It just makes me next in line.'

'Dad, this is about Grandma,' I said. 'She died. You're OK.'

'No,' he said. 'She's better off where she is now. I'm just stuck being death on wheels down here.'

'The viewing is on Sunday,' I said. 'At Galt's Funeral Parlour. You should stop by there. I think you need to sign some papers and find out what time to show up and stuff.'

'Well, I've got to say,' he said, looking up at the sky, then out across the maze of pens, looking around at everything through his wet eyes except at me, 'this town has been nothing but a crock of bad luck. Your mom nearly killed me. Then she broke my heart a few times. All the help you gave me seems to have backfired. And after the Thanksgiving Day massacre, I think I've worn out my welcome around here,' he concluded. 'I'll bury my mom and beat it, before your mom's aim improves and the police put me in a beggar's grave.'

'I don't want to hurt you,' I said. 'You know I've been trying my best to help.'

'I know you wouldn't hurt me,' he replied, 'not intentionally. You just got to realize that a guy like me only gets a hurtin' put on him when he tries to get better. I'm really much happier when I'm not trying to improve myself. You know what I mean?'

I'm not sure I did. And I wasn't sure what to say. I stood there wondering if he could explain himself more clearly or if he would confuse me even more because I just couldn't believe that everyone didn't want to get better. That's all I ever wanted to do – get better.

'Do you have any money?' he asked. 'I need to take a bath, and the YMCA charges five bucks, and I'm flat broke, and I'm out of smokes too.'

I had Grandma's money in my pocket, but I had her words with me too. *Nothing for them.*

'Dad, go by the house and take a bath,' I said. 'The door's wide open, and Grandma had a few cigarettes left over.'

'Fran really hates me,' he said, starting up again. 'I didn't touch her.'

'You scare her, Dad,' I said. 'She wants a normal life, and you are about the last thing in the world I'd call normal.'

'Guess I'm more like a comet,' he said. 'I'll leave town after the funeral, but I'll circle back someday. Maybe next time I'll be on top of the world. Maybe I'll have won the lottery and be so rich you all will be begging to spend some time with me.'

'Dad, why don't you go get that bath now? Mom's working a wedding, and I'm going over to a friend's house, so you can be alone there.'

'Can I give you a lift?' he asked, rubbing his side.

That reminded me. 'Did you ever stop by the hospital and get your medicine?' I asked.

'Haven't had a chance,' he said. 'I've been pretty busy.'

'Well, remember to go by the funeral parlour,' I said.

'Don't worry,' he replied. 'I think I can remember that.'

'Are you sure?'

'Come on,' he said, pointing to his motor-cycle. 'I'll give you a ride.'

As soon as I rang the doorbell, Mrs Lapp answered as if she was expecting me.

'Why, Joey,' she said cheerfully, 'I'm so happy to see you again. I was a little too worked up the last time we spoke. I haven't changed my mind about the schooling, but I said some personal things about you and your family I regret. I owe you an apology. Forgive me?'

'W.W.J.D.?' I asked.

'I hope he'd forgive me,' she said.

'Sure he will,' I said. 'And I do too. A few grumpy words can't rattle me for ever.'

'You've been very kind,' she said. 'I'll miss

you around here. How about one last W.W.J.D.? to you. Make it a good one.'

I did. 'Well, my grandmother just died this morning, and I'm hoping that he'll let her into heaven despite her smoking, drinking, cursing and sometimes mean-as-a-snake behaviour.'

Mrs Lapp looked up into the air, held her hands together in prayer, and closed her eyes. 'I'm quite sure she is looking down on us right now,' she said softly.

I looked up at the sky and waved my big wild happy wave like I'm lost on a desert island and I'm waving to an aeroplane passing overhead.

'You can pray,' Mrs Lapp suggested.

'I like to wave,' I said. 'When I think of God, I always think of a great big yellow smiley face – the kind with the winking eyes and happy smile. Sometimes I just wink up at God and say "Hi – have a good day."'

After a moment I heard Olivia tapping my way. 'Hi,' she said to me. Then she turned to her mom. 'Can we have some privacy, please?'

'Five minutes,' Mrs Lapp replied. 'Then we're off to our mother–daughter fellowship meeting.'

As soon as Mrs Lapp was out of earshot, Olivia whispered. 'Hey, did you come up with a way for us to see *Godspell*?'

'No,' I said. 'I came by to let you know my grandma died but that you didn't kill her. She was dying long before you told her I was your new friend.'

'Are you sure she didn't die from a delayed reaction?'

'I'm sure,' I replied.

'Well, I'm sorry,' she said.

Suddenly Mrs Lapp hollered to me from the kitchen. 'Joey, do you want to take one of these Key lime pies home with you?'

'No, thank you,' I answered. 'There's nobody at home to eat it.'

Olivia pulled me closer. 'That blowout your family had yesterday scared some sense into my mom. She called Dad on the road and they are already talking about boarding school. Keep your fingers crossed.'

'That's great for you,' I said.

'Sorry I used you as the sacrificial lamb,' she said. 'As you can see, my mom can't stay mad for long. But I can. If you don't get me to *Godspell*, you'll be joining your grandma.'

'You are so mean,' I said.

'Not really,' she replied. 'Now, what's your plan? Just because your grandma died doesn't mean you get to wiggle out of your half of the deal.'

'Still thinkin',' I said.

'You better be thinking,' she said. 'Or I'll track you down and make your life even more miserable.'

'OK,' I said. 'Give me a little time. I'll come up with a plan.' And I walked away thinking, but I had no idea what to do, so I just kept walking and making the rounds of all my JOEY WAS HERE labels because I didn't want to go home and bump into the funeral parlour people taking Grandma away, and I didn't want to be there if Dad decided to take a bath. I just kept walking. People were already putting up Christmas lights, and I hadn't gotten over Thanksgiving yet. I'm just stuck in a rut, I said to myself, and I don't like it.

12.

Socks and Shoes

I really didn't look forward to waking up in the morning, because it was going to be the beginning of another day I didn't understand. I usually love Saturdays. But not this one. I could only think of Grandma, and now she would only be part of my past.

Then suddenly my present was calling me – Pablo and Pablita were licking my face as if my head were a bowl of dog food. They were hungry *now*.

I jumped up. 'I am so sorry,' I said to them. 'Soooooo sorry.' The last time I fed them was when I gave them the turkey jerky.

'Let's get some breakfast.'

I pulled on the play clothes I had been wearing and put the dogs in my backpack. It was easier to carry them than to put them on a leash and poke along behind them. When I left my bedroom, I noticed Mom's door was closed. I looked away and tried not to stare at Grandma's empty couch. But I couldn't help it. 'I'll see you tomorrow,' I said, and jerked my head away.

'Let's go,' I whispered to Pablita as I opened the front door and we ran down the steps. 'You can ask Pablo, but I am usually much more responsible than this. I mean, once I locked him in the glove compartment and forgot him for a while, and once I threw a dart and it pierced his ear by mistake, but otherwise he has had a very good life with me. Honest.' And as we headed for the All-American Discount Grocery Store, I pointed out the little gnomes that someone had stacked up one on top of the other like a gnome totem pole. I pointed out the coldest spot on the ice-factory wall. We ran under the railroad bridge where the homeless man was asking for money. We ran away but turned around and ran back and gave him five dollars from Grandma's money because even dogs don't like anyone to go hungry, and then we ran away again. We ran over to the Goodwill box, and I tucked each dog under my arm, and we all peeked our heads into the bin. There was a nice pair of ladies' shoes in there, and I grabbed them just in case I saw the woman who only wore socks.

There were also some boys' clothes that somebody must have kept in their attic for a lifetime. I had seen pictures of kids from about a hundred years ago, and they were all dressed like small adults in nice pants and dress shoes with shirts and ties and suit jackets. They looked ready to do something important with themselves, as if they could walk into a business and be the boss. They looked smart and serious, like they had something more on their minds than video games and sports and all kinds of kid stuff that really didn't matter all that much when you thought about it. Mom dressed me in jeans and T-shirts and sneakers, and I walked around as if all I was prepared to do was play in a sandbox. Adults are always trying to keep their kids from growing up too fast, but most of the kids I know want to grow up fast so they can get away from their nutty parents who wear jeans and T-shirts all day and look like big scary kids who have refused to grow up. Then it occurred to me that I needed to buy some nice-looking serious clothes so other people would take me as seriously as I wanted to take myself. Maybe that was my big Saturday thought – to look as grown-up as I had become.

Pablo and Pablita started barking again, and so we ran straight for the discount grocery store. I got a shopping cart by the front door and set my backpack in it. 'Now be quiet,' I said, 'or we'll get kicked out.' First I bought a box of dog biscuits and a box of dried dog food. Then I poured it all into the backpack and mostly zipped it up. Right away they sounded as if they were eating each other. 'Be nice,' I said into the opening, 'there's enough for everyone.' They didn't quiet down, so I parked them next to the stale bread section and ran back over to the store manager's office.

I knocked on his open door. 'It's me, Mr Helpful,' I sang. 'I'm here to clean up the store.'

'Hey Mr Helpful,' the manager said. 'Where've you been? We missed you around here. The place is a mess without you.'

'Well, have no fear,' I said. 'I'm back on the job.'

'What's that stuck to your forehead?' he asked.

I reached up and peeled the I'M THE LEFT-OVERS label off my head. 'Just a joke,' I explained.

And so I began to go up and down the aisles and rearrange the cans and put all the things that ended up in the wrong places into the right places. I rotated the bottles and jars so they all faced out, built castle walls out of the toilet paper rolls, organized the razor blades by brand and style, and restacked the little pyramids of oranges and apples. And doing all this work was a good thing because I didn't think of Mom or Dad or Booth or Grandma or anyone. I didn't even think of me. All I did was keep my fingers moving as quickly as possible and work at putting all the misplaced things back in their proper places. I even bumped into the lady with socks and gave her the shoes. She didn't say a word to me but slipped them onto her feet and kept right on walking down the two-for-one aisle until I noticed they were on the wrong feet. I wanted to creep up behind her and quickly switch them around, but I didn't. You just can't help everyone. But it made me feel so much better to see shoes go over socks and cans all in a row with their puffed-out chests and red-cheeked labels, and suddenly I felt as though I lived in a world that I ruled and I knew exactly where I fit in. At least for a little while.

I took a victory lap around the store, and when I finished, I stood in front of the manager's open door and looked up into the security camera TVs. I saw a pretty shabby-looking boy staring up into the air. I looked like I was on the shelf with all the dented-up cans that were sold at half price, and when people get you for half price, they treat you like you're half as good, and I didn't want any part of that.

I knocked on the manager's door.

'Are you finished, Mr Helpful?' he asked.

'Yeah,' I said. 'I think I'm finished for good. I'm tired of cleaning up after other people.'

'Well, I'll miss you,' he said. 'But I understand how it is. You fix things up, and as soon as you turn your back, people make a mess of everything you've done.'

'At my house you don't even have to turn your back,' I said. 'My family likes to make a mess right in front of your face.'

He nodded.

'See you around,' I said. I hooked my wiggling backpack over my shoulder and walked out the sliding doors and on up to the top of Queen Street, where I caught the bus to the Fruitville Mall. I hadn't ever been shopping for clothes by myself before, so I just strolled through the stores looking at the mannequins until I found one I liked. He was dressed in khaki pants with a light blue shirt and navy blue blazer with a striped tie. He had on paisley socks and brown penny loafers and a brown belt, and I thought if he had something to say, people would listen. If he said, 'Put down that knife,' Mom would put it down. If he said, 'Straighten up and get a job,' Dad would pull himself together, get a job, and start acting his age and not his shoe size. And if he had told Grandma to stop smoking cigarettes and breathe some fresh air once in a while, she'd still be alive.

I got a man to help me, and I told him I wanted that exact outfit plus underwear, and he took me and the dogs back to a fitting room and kept bringing me different sizes until we got them right. I kept on my new outfit and threw my old clothes into the trash. I stood on the fitting platform and looked into the three-way mirror and rotated my head back and forth and thought I looked smart from every angle. If the mirror was a door that someone opened, they would see a very handsome, very serious, very thoughtful young man. And they would say, 'May I help you?' And I would say, 'Yes, you may help me.'

Sometimes Grandma and I would go to a toy store downtown and play with all the toys, and Grandma didn't care if I opened the boxes and took the stuff out and played with it even though she knew we'd never buy it. Once we sat down at a table for tiny kids and opened the Dating Game board game, and I remembered not dressing my guy character too well, and Grandma always had really stylish-looking girls who were waiting for a date, but when my guy showed up at their front door, Grandma had the girl slam the door in my face and in a huffy voice said, 'I ordered a *hunk* not a *chump*!' Even then Grandma told me I was going to have to start looking like the great kid I wanted to be instead of the ratty kid I was. She may have hurt my feelings, but it turns out she was right. I wanted to look like I ruled the whole world. And if nothing else, I wanted to look like I ruled Joey's world.

When I paid the clerk in cash, he said, 'You look like you're getting ready to do something important.'

'Thanks,' I said. 'I am.'

As we left the store, I said to Pablo and Pablita, 'It's time to take the bull by the horns, as Grandma would say.' We caught the bus downtown to the Central Market and walked up to the ticket window at the Fulton Opera House. 'Two of your best seats, please,' I said. I gave him ninety dollars, and the man put the tickets in an envelope and slipped them to me through the glass slot. I opened my jacket and slipped the envelopes into the inside pocket, then marched up the street.

'Olivia gave Grandma a feel-good send-off,' I said to myself. 'Now it's our turn to give Olivia a feel-good send-off.'

Only I wasn't sure yet how I'd get around Mrs Lapp. But Saturday wasn't over. I still had some more thinking to do, and I was feeling very sharp, very confident, very powerful, and I strutted down the street looking as if I owned the entire town, except that I had two yapping Chihuahuas sticking out of my backpack barking at everyone and everything we passed. They kept me humble.

13

Tug-of-War

'I did something I think I'm going to regret,' Mom said.

I didn't have time to imagine what she might regret. We were in the funeral parlour, and I had been by myself alone in a room with Grandma for about an hour. I had rearranged her hair abut a dozen times, and then I'd push some lipstick on her, then some more and more, until I thought it was too wide, or too shiny, and then I'd take a tissue and rub it around and lick the tissue and rub some more and start all over again. I was a nervous wreck, and I was waiting for

Dad because he had left a message at the funeral parlour telling me to be a little early because he wanted to meet me here before Mom arrived, but he hadn't shown up. Even though it was cold outside, I had opened a window because I thought I could at least hear his motorcycle from far away and I would know he was coming. I looked at the reflection of myself in the mirror above a little table where there was a vase of lilies and a small book where anybody who came to the viewing could write their name. I wrote mine, *Mister Joey P. Pigza*, and then I wrote *Mrs Frances Pigza* and below it *Mr Carter Pigza* because I knew it was just going to be the three of us. Pablo and Pablita were not allowed to attend. I had asked, but pets at funeral parlours were against regulations because they might 'upset the grieving', Mr Galt explained. He had never met my parents.

I fussed with trying to straighten out my necktie because I wasn't sure how to tie one, and when I took it off to go to bed, I made the mistake of untying it, and now it came out looking more like a knot you hang someone with. Standing in front of the open window had made me cold on the inside, even though I had on my new shirt and jacket and matching pants, new underwear, new socks, and shoes. I kept walking circles around the coffin, and once I went into the bathroom and found a book left in the toilet stall called *The Final Days*. I took it with me back to where Grandma was laid out and read a few pages and the jacket. It was a story with young people worrying about what will happen to them when they die because they know they will be judged by God and either get blasted up to heaven or sent straight down to hell. All they think about is death all day long instead of thinking about all the good things that could happen here on earth right now. They have a lot to worry about, and they seem afraid that if they don't do enough good deeds, they are cooked. It was hard enough for me worrying about Santa Claus and wondering if I was on his naughty or nice list that he was always checking twice. If I had to worry every minute of each day over whether I was going to die and burn in hell for all eternity or go to heaven and be happy for ever, I would be a nervous wreck. I had to put down the book because the more I read, the jumpier I became and the more I wanted to run home and hide under the bed with Pablo and Pablita.

That's when the door opened and Mom marched in and said she had done something she regretted, and I was just staring at her like Grandma's little zombie.

'Well, aren't you going to ask what I'm going to regret?' Mom asked.

'Sorry,' I replied. 'My mind drifted.'

'I just bailed your father out of jail,' she said, shaking her head as if she was surprised by her own words. 'The reason he isn't here is he was on his way and stopped in at the discount grocery store and was arrested there for shoplifting some doughnuts.'

'Doughnuts?' I said a little too loudly. I was more confused about what he stole than about the thought that he would steal.

'Yeah, doughnuts,' she repeated. 'He was stealing snacks for the little reception we're having after your grandmother's service.'

'Well, thanks for bailing him out,' I said.

'Booth thought I was nuts,' she said. 'And I can't disagree with him. This whole deal today would go a lot smoother if Carter stayed behind bars.'

'Then why'd you do it?' I asked.

'I guess I felt I owed him one after I tried to throw that knife right between his eyes. I mean, that's not exactly a good thing to do. What do you think?'

I wanted to ask her what she thought of my new outfit, but at that moment Dad entered the room running as if he was trying to break an Olympic record. He passed us, dodged the coffin in the middle of the room, and finally slowed down when he hit the far wall with his outstretched hands. 'What a morning!' he shouted when he turned around.

'What a moron!' Mom said, mimicking him. 'I can't believe you stole some dough-nuts. How low can you get?'

I knew they were going to argue. I was ready for that. I just didn't know what they were going to argue about because they always went over and over the old subjects about who was mean to who first, and who was irresponsible, and who was a no-good drunk, and who was a loser, and who was a crummy parent, and who took better or worse care of me or whatever. I mean, I was ready for some sort of blowout because by now I had figured the funeral was where the seventh bad thing would happen. Still, I was not ready for what happened next. The only person who was ready was Grandma, and that was because she was already dead.

From across the room they began to stare at each other like contenders in a heavy-weight prizefight. Dad was in one corner of the room jerking his head back and forth and cracking his knuckles like he was getting psyched up to kill someone. Mom was in the other corner just glowering at him with her X-ray look of death. I was stuck like the referee in the middle. But it was an odd fight because the only prize was Grandma, and she was already down for the count – decked out in an open wooden coffin on a small table.

The fight began when Mom said these words: 'This coffin is a disgrace. You have insulted your mother's memory.'

'There's not a thing wrong with this coffin,' Dad said. 'A lot of people are buried in a plain wooden box.'

'Yeah,' she shot back. 'I can think of a few

– dogs, cats, birds, hamsters – *pets*! You are burying your mother as if she were a pet. Why don't you just bury her in the backyard?'

'Actually,' he said, 'I am. She'll go into St Mary's Cemetery, and you can see her from the house.'

'You know that's not what I meant,' she said. 'I meant that you should bury her with some dignity.'

'I think she looks fine,' Dad said. 'In fact, I think she looks more dignified in death than in life.'

'You cheap creep. You could have bought her a good coffin,' Mom snarled. 'And a new dress. And had her properly laid out.'

I wanted to tell Mom that Grandma had picked out the dress from her chest of old dresses and that the funeral people had cleaned it and ironed it and I had done the make-up and hair. But I didn't want to get more in the middle than I already was.

'You haven't given a cent towards it,' he said. 'I'll have to sell my motorcycle to pay for the plot.'

'Well, if you had a life, you would have been able to pay for something decent.'

'Stop it,' Dad said. 'Just back off.'

'No,' Mom said, stepping towards him.

'If you don't like it, you can leave,' Dad said.

'I'm not leaving without her,' Mom replied. 'I'll give her a proper burial and not put her in the ground in some overgrown cigar box.' She reached in and ran her arms under Grandma and began to lift her out like a fireman hoisting someone over their shoulder.

'She's fine,' Dad said. 'Just fine. It doesn't matter if it's a wooden box or solid gold. We all go to the same place.' He reached over Mom's shoulders and pushed Grandma back into the coffin.

'Well, she's not going to show up at the pearly gates looking like she just checked out of the poorhouse.' Mom grabbed Grandma by the shoulders and lifted.

Dad pushed her back into the coffin again. 'Stop it,' he said.

Mom ran to the head of the coffin and got a grip on Grandma's shoulders and began to pull her out. Dad grabbed Grandma by the ankles and they were yanking on her and I just stood there with my mouth hanging open watching Grandma being pulled back and forth like an elastic band. The next thing I knew Grandma's shoes came off in Dad's hands and he tumbled backwards and Mom stumbled back into a chair and the coffin slid off the table and hit the floor and Granny flopped out onto the carpet. I screamed.

'Now look what you've done!' Dad hollered.

'This is all your fault,' Mom spit back. 'If you had treated your own mother decently, then we wouldn't be in this mess.'

'Stop it!' I yelled.

'Quiet, Joey,' Dad snapped.

'Joey, go outside,' Mom ordered. 'I need to speak to your father alone.'

'No,' I said defiantly. I knelt down and put my face on Grandma's chest. I thought maybe her heart would start beating again and she'd come back to life like in *The Return of the Mummy* and pop up and knock some sense into both my parents. She had knocked plenty of sense into me. And even though I pressed and pressed my face against her and begged her to come back and be with me, she didn't. She was just as cold and wrinkled as if she had been carved out of an old log. And the next thing I knew Mom had pulled me off Grandma and was pressing me against her belly with one hand while reaching over my head with her other to try and slap Dad, who had his arms up in front of his face, and he was doing a jig and hollering, 'Don't get me started! Don't you get me worked up, or you'll be in the coffin with her!'

I broke away from Mom and bolted towards the door, but before running off I just shouted about as loud as I possibly could, 'What's the matter with you? Are you as hopeless as Grandma said? Don't you know she is going to be cremated and that they always use a wooden coffin for that? And everything has already been paid for anyway! She used her own money.'

Then I ran out the door.

'I'll speak to you later, young man!' Mom shouted. But she didn't come after me because she had already turned towards Dad and they continued to blame each other for everything bad that had ever happened between them. With the window open in the funeral parlour, I could hear them as I passed by. I wanted to stop and stick my head in the window and yell, 'Grow up!' and make them sit quietly in chairs facing opposite corners until they could control themselves. But I knew they wouldn't listen to me. They didn't want my help. They always did just what they wanted to do, and when things turned out badly, they made up excuses to try and wiggle out of the mess they'd made for everyone around them – which means mostly me. I expect my dad to behave badly, but when Mom is bad too, it really upsets me because I count on her. I keep trying to make some sense out of what they do, but they've got me all mixed up, and I can't figure them out to save my life. So I'm pretty sure I should forget about them and just think about what *I* should do. Even though, as I ran away, I really wanted to turn around and try to fix things up just one more time.

When I arrived at the Lapps', I decided that when Mrs Lapp had said she secretly needed my help, it really meant that I had to secretly help her understand Olivia. I'm sure she didn't think of it that way. I figured I had to make her see what Olivia saw inside herself. That was the only way they were going to see eye to eye. If I had tried to sneak Olivia out of the house and we were caught by her mother, I would only look like one more crazy Pigza and make things worse between them. So I got my courage up, straightened the noose around my neck, and rang the front doorbell.

When Mrs Lapp opened the door, I was standing there holding a single rose I had picked out from a bucket of them at the Mini Mart. I had sniffed them all and made sure this one smelled the strongest. It didn't look so good, but Olivia was blind so how it looked didn't matter.

'Hello, Mrs Lapp,' I said.

'Hello, Joey,' she replied. 'You look very handsomely dressed this afternoon. What is the special occasion?'

'I just came from my grandmother's funeral. And now I'm here to ask permission to take Olivia to see *Godspell*,' I said directly.

She stood there for a moment, weighing something in her mind, then said, 'That's very thoughtful of you, Joey. But you know how I feel about religion used as entertainment. Especially *Godspell*. I saw the poster downtown, and Jesus was wearing a Superman costume and a clown nose. Joey, that is not my idea of religious respect.'

'I know how you feel about *Godspell*,' I said, sounding as respectful as I could. 'But do you know how Olivia feels about it?'

She turned to look at Olivia, who was standing behind her. 'Olivia feels the same way as I do,' she assured me. 'Right, Olivia?'

'Not really,' Olivia said. 'I love *Godspell*. I have the tape. The kids in church were listening to it, and they made me a copy.'

I removed the tickets from inside my jacket. 'Please let her come with me,' I said as nicely as I could. 'I don't think I'll see much of her in the future, and this would be kind of a goodbye present.'

'Please, Mom?' Olivia asked. 'I just love the music. I didn't even know Jesus was wearing a clown nose and Superman costume until you just said it. Please?'

Mrs Lapp looked at Olivia, then she looked at me.

'W.W.J.D.?' I shouted when I caught her eye.

She looked up at the blue belly of the sky, then down at me. 'He'd let Joey take Olivia,' she said.

Olivia squealed. I wanted to tell Mrs Lapp that I had helped her see the light, but didn't. I pressed my lips together tighter than ever because if I opened my mouth, I might mess things up by saying too much. So I just said to myself, Thanks for the advice, Grandma.

'I need to get ready,' Olivia said. Mrs Lapp followed her into her bedroom.

I waited in the living room for a while, sniffing the rose and staring at the big clock that called out the time every five minutes. Then Mrs Lapp and Olivia returned. Olivia was all dressed up like a bridesmaid in a long, shiny green gown with a very large white bow on her back. She had a beautiful jade cross around her neck, and her hair was pulled back into a bun.

She looked so great, I thought she might call me a chump.

'For you,' I said, and pressed the rose into her hand.

She sniffed it. 'A black rose,' she said. 'My favourite.'

Even though I had accidentally pricked her finger with one of the rose thorns and a little drop of blood slid into her palm, she didn't say anything mean.

'You two better get going,' said Mrs Lapp. Olivia started for her room to get her cane and pads.

'Don't,' I called out to her. 'You can hang onto my arm.'

'Are you sure about this?' Mrs Lapp asked.

'Yes,' I replied. 'I'll only cross at the corner, and then I'll look both ways first.'

'Well, OK,' she said.

Once Olivia and I began to stroll down the sidewalk, I looked over at her and whispered, 'Don't you think this is better than sneaking out?'

'It is,' she replied. 'But it would be cool too if I had to climb out my window.'

'Yeah, but it wouldn't be cool if we were caught,' I said.

And I think we would have been caught. Because when I stopped at the corner and looked both ways, I saw Mrs Lapp's car sneaking up the road behind us.

When we arrived at the theatre, I held the door open for her and gave the usher our tickets. He led us upstairs and down a hall past a row of narrow doors. Then he stopped in front of one. He checked the door and the number on our tickets and directed us inside.

'You have to describe everything to me,' she said. 'Where are we sitting?'

'In our own private little balcony,' I replied, looking around with my mouth open. 'It's very nice. I feel like we are inside a red-velvet and gold jewellery box.'

I put her hands on the brass railing and lined the chair up behind her. 'Now, turn your head a bit to your left and down, and you'll be facing right at the centre of the stage.'

The orchestra began to warm up, and all the different instruments sounded like crazy musical traffic, and then suddenly the lights dimmed and the curtain opened and a line of singers came out dressed like Raggedy Ann and Raggedy Andy and a bunch of beat-up Goodwill dolls. And as they began to sing, Olivia sang along with them. She couldn't see a thing but she knew all the words. I could see, and watched for a moment as the players chased each other back and forth. But I wasn't singing. Instead, the only words I remembered were from Grandma and they didn't sound like music. But they were loud. She had said that from behind her curtain the whole bunch of us Pigzas were like our own play coming and going and making a mess out of everything. Now things were just getting worse. Grandma was dead. Dad was taking off. And Mom was *mad*. Her last words were, 'I'll speak to you later.' So while everyone in the opera house was thinking about John the Baptist and Jesus and good people and bad people and heaven and hell, I was thinking about Mom in my own house, with me.

At intermission I needed to move around just to get away from myself. 'I'll be right back,' I said to Olivia. I stood up and went out our own door and down the hall, then down a set of steps to the men's room. When I came out, I wanted to see where we were sitting from the floor, so I walked down the centre aisle. I looked up and saw the side of Olivia's face. Then when I turned around my eyes nearly bugged out. There was Mrs Lapp sitting in the middle of a row. I got as close to her as I could and waved until she saw me. I pointed up to Olivia, and she smiled. Then she held one finger up over her lips. I nodded. I wouldn't tell, not because I thought Mrs Lapp wanted to keep it a secret that she came but because she wanted to be the first one to share that secret with Olivia.

After the show it was still light outside, and Olivia and I walked home. She was so happy and it made me feel good, because watching someone else be happy was so much better than thinking about how unhappy Mom was with me.

'I probably won't see you for a while,' I said when we arrived at her house. 'How will I write you?'

'There's a braille typewriter at the public library,' she said. 'Just ask for it. Or better yet, write. But use lots of swear words so when the church ladies read it to me, they'll get flustered.'

I smiled. 'I'll miss you,' I said.

I was going to open the door, but she stood in the way and stuck her arms straight out and leaned her face and lips forward. I wasn't sure what to do because I never kissed a girl before other than my mom and grandma.

'Hurry and kiss me,' she whispered. 'If my mom catches us, she'll send me to a convent.'

I stuck my arms straight out and stuck my

lips way out and closed my eyes and figured we were lined up properly. I inched forward, and she did too. My forehead hit her chin, and then I stood up on my tiptoes, and she bent her knees, and we kissed for about as long as it takes to blink. And by the time Mrs Lapp opened the front door and winked at me, Olivia and I were just standing side by side holding hands and smiling. And Mrs Lapp was smiling too. Something was making her eyes shine.

'Joey,' she said, 'even though we've decided that Olivia is going away, you can still come by and ring my doorbell, OK?'

'Don't worry about that,' I said. 'I love to ring doorbells.'

Then she bent down and whispered in my ear. 'You can always be my secret helper.'

Then I just bit my lip and waved a tiny wave like a sad fish waving goodbye and drifted slowly all the way home.

I could tell Mom had been on the warpath. She had already ripped down Grandma's shower curtain and piled up all of Grandma's clothes and bathroom things into grocery bags for Goodwill. She had stacked all the couch cushions on the front porch and had dragged the couch out to the front door but hadn't got it through just yet.

'Where have you been?' she asked angrily. She had a broom and was sweeping up a pile of old cigarette butts Grandma had tossed into the corner behind the couch. 'I've been looking for you everywhere.'

'That's my business,' I said.

'Well, things are going to change around here, young man.'

'I hope so,' I said.

'First help me drag this smelly couch outside. It stinks.'

I grabbed one end and grunted and lifted it up over the threshold of the doorway, and Mom gave it a push, then another. I jumped out of the way, and she kept pushing until it thumped down the front steps. Then she picked up one end and heaved it onto the sidewalk. I threw the pillows from the porch.

'So,' she started up again looking just as wild-eyed as the day she drove the broom handle through Dad's motorcycle spokes. 'Where have you been? With your father?'

"Where have *you* been?' I asked right back. 'With your boyfriend?'

'He's gone,' she said without much emotion. 'Said he didn't want to sink down to *my* level. Said I was bad karma, whatever that is,' she remarked. 'I can't blame him. All he wanted was a fairy-tale life, and all we gave him was a nightmare. Well, maybe it's for the best,' she said, but her face looked disappointed.

'And I have to do what is best for me,' I said.

'Well, tell me,' she said with her hands on her hips, 'tell me, Mister Joey P. Pigza, just what is best for you?'

'First,' I said. 'I want to get back to regular school. I want to go back to Mrs Lucchina's class.'

'Oh no you don't,' she said, shaking her head back and forth. 'No. You are doing so much better at Mrs Lapp's.'

'I've got news for you,' I said. 'Mrs Lapp kicked me out of her school. And not because of anything I did. She saw that huge scene you and Dad pitched on the front steps at Thanksgiving. After that she decided that maybe my family was too

274

messed up and I'd be a bad influence on Olivia. And now she's sending Olivia off to boarding school. And believe me, I wish I was going with her so I wouldn't have to see you again.'

'Don't speak to me that way, young man,' she snapped. 'I think you owe me an apology.'

'Can I get back to you on that?' I blurted out, shouting the one thing she *didn't* want to hear, and stomped into my room.

'That's right,' she hollered. 'You go to your room, and you stay there and I want you to think about your behaviour.'

'That's all I ever think about,' I yelled back. 'And I'm so tired of thinking about my behaviour, I've started to think about *yours!*'

She whipped open my bedroom door. 'Do me a favour,' she said angrily. 'If you come up with any more ways to improve me, keep them to yourself!' Then she slammed the door so hard, Dad's silencer fell off the wall and onto my pillow, then bounced off onto the floor. I picked it up and opened the window and threw it outside. Then I closed the window and locked it. I didn't need a souvenir to know what it felt like to be squished between Mom and Dad.

I undressed and carefully hung up my new clothes. I buttoned all the buttons on the shirt. I made sure the creases in the pants were perfectly lined up. I unknotted my tie and draped it over a hanger. I bent down and used one of my socks to buff my shoes. Then I put on my pyjamas and sat down on the side of my bed. I reached down to the floor and picked up my label marker and spelled out JOEY. Then I pressed it on my forehead. I turned off the lights, and when I climbed into bed, I lay down like a corpse with my hands against my sides and my feet straight out. I didn't want to be dead. But the idea of being alone in a quiet wooden box was a pretty nice thought. It was peaceful. Then I heard Mom calling Booth on the telephone. Then I heard her calling him a 'quitter' and some other worse names, then I heard the phone smashing against the wall and Pablo and Pablita running for cover. Grandma was right. He didn't stick around once he saw what a bunch of nuts we were.

Then I heard her open a kitchen cabinet, and the clinking of glasses. In a moment she plopped down into a chair. 'I'm sorry,' she said to the dogs. 'I'm not upset with you, just myself. I don't know why I was thinking it would take a man to pull us together. I guess I was just hoping for something easy to happen around here.'

We all were.

14

W.W.J.D.?

When I woke up, I thought Grandma was alive again. The sucking sound of the wind tugging back and forth on the plastic sheeting over the front door sounded like her laboured breathing. The morning light was just coming around. I rolled over and lowered my feet to the floor. Mom must have let the dogs into my room when I was sleeping because Pablo and Pablita were cuddled up on their beanbag chair.

I tiptoed out of my room and peeked in Mom's room. She was still asleep, and I didn't want to wake her up. I got ready for school as quietly as possible. When I finished, I looked into the mirror. It was like a big crystal ball, and the only thing in it was me. The friendly me, I thought, with JOEY on my forehead so everyone would know my name right away.

I patted Pablo and Pablita on their little heads. Grandma knew it all along. Pablo was a dog. Now he was a dog with a dog friend and protected by Mrs Lapp's D.O.G. medal, which I had snapped onto his collar. And now it was time for me to get back to my class and meet those kids who didn't know yet what a great friend I was going to be to them.

I poured the rest of the dog food out of my backpack into an old shoe Pablo liked to chew on, and that kept the dogs busy while I tiptoed out the back door. I walked across our yard and through the cemetery. I passed the funeral parlour on the way to school. I knew Grandma would be proud of me for doing what was best for me and nobody else. I looked up into the sky. Her big face was still smiling down on me. 'This is good thing number one,' I said to her. 'From now on I'm just counting good things.'

Then I heard a motorcycle. Maybe it was Dad, maybe not. But just the growl of that motor echoing off the buildings sounded like an argument hollering back and forth at itself. I just wish Dad could shout out something good about himself sometime. Maybe that would echo back and surprise him.

I stopped in at the Mini Mart to get a Yoo-Hoo and a muffin. I still had about a hundred dollars. I thought, After school I'm going to the bank and open a college fund. Grandma was right. I didn't need to make money by being an experiment. I stood in front of the store and watched the town wake up. Lights came on in houses. I could see shadows against the curtains. Everyone had to wake up to somebody. Everyone had to wake up to themselves. And I was wondering who I might be if I didn't have the nutty family I had. And then I realized it didn't matter where I came from. It was where I was going that counted. And as long as I helped myself, I'd be going in the right direction.

I looked down the sidewalk towards the school. A couple of kids were raising the flag. Teachers were pulling in the driveway. The supply trucks were around the back delivering food. The crossing guard was putting on her orange vest. And suddenly I saw Mom get out of a cab and start towards me.

Her words reached me before her arms. 'I knew you'd be here,' she said.

'Where else would I be? It's a school day,' I said.

'Do you want me to come in with you?' she asked.

'No,' I replied. 'I know where I'm going.'

'Well, I'll call the principal and set everything up.'

'Thanks,' I said, and turned away.

'Joey, I want you to move on,' she said. 'Really, I do. But you don't have to move on without me.'

'I know,' I said, 'but I don't want to be like you and Dad doing the same scary stuff over and over again. Dad goes in circles. You have your ups and downs, and I just want to go forward.'

'Then give me a kiss before you blast off,' she replied. She bent down and ran her fingers under the lapels of my jacket. 'You look very handsome,' she said. 'Very grown up.'

I kissed her on one cheek. 'Are you still mad at me?' I asked.

'How can I be mad at such a handsome boy?' she said.

I grinned. 'I look like a *hunk*,' I whispered.

'You're my little *hunk*,' she said.

I kissed her on the other cheek.

Then quickly she reached out and ripped the JOEY label off my forehead.

'Ouch!' I shouted.

'I'm your mom,' she said. 'You don't need a label for me.'

I kissed her again. 'One question. Did you get Grandma back in the coffin?'

'Yes,' she said.

'Did you get her shoes on again?'

'Can I get back to you on that?' she asked.

I grinned because I liked that she was imitating *me*. 'OK,' I said, stepping away. 'But I'll be a little late. I have a lot of catching up to do.'

'When you get home, I'll order Chinese takeout.'

'I'd like that,' I said, and took a couple more steps.

'One more thing,' she added. 'I really like Pablita. It's great to have another girl in the house.'

'Yeah,' I said. 'I like girls.' Then I turned and ran the rest of the way down the sidewalk and up the front steps. I glanced back, and she was still standing there with one hand on her hip. Then I turned and pressed my hand against the wooden door. I could feel the worn spot where so many hands had pushed against it. I liked that spot.

'W.W.J.D.?' I asked myself.

Then I answered. 'He'd help himself. That's just what that smart kid would do. Help himself.' I gave the door a push. I was in, and everything outside faded behind me. I was in where I belonged.